# SILENCE HAS MANY FACES

## Frances Day

First published 2023 by Frances Day

Produced by Independent Ink
independentink.com.au

Cover design by Catucci Design
Edited by Wordplay Editing Services
Internal design by Independent Ink
Typeset in 12/18 pt Adobe Garamond Pro by Post Pre-press Group, Brisbane
Cover images: Background: ChristianB/istockphoto.com; Barbed wire: Best Content Production Group/istockphoto.com

ISBN 978-0-646-88497-4 (paperback)
ISBN 978-0-6486294-1-2 (epub)

To Lucy and Ash, my four legged companions,
for the love and laughter you bring into my life.

Choose your silences wisely.
They can both protect and injure.

ANONYMOUS

## Chapter One

# Jane

I had never thought of silence as something that could be palpable; it was so thick and heavy, I thought we were all going to suffocate. I glanced at Mum, who was staring at the two men sitting calmly on the couch unaware that they had interrupted our usually relaxed Saturday morning.

Saturday was our family day. A day we spent together, away from the demands of everyone and everything else. Uncle Arthur sometimes joined us, though most often not. He preferred the solitude of the bush and the company of his four dogs.

The morning began as usual, with me creeping (I made too much noise, or so I had been told – repeatedly – hence the creeping) out to the kitchen to make my first coffee for the day. The kettle was still warm, so someone had been there before me. Maybe Uncle Arthur? He sometimes moved the cattle early and would let himself into the house for an early morning coffee. He was as silent as a shadow, so no one would have heard him – least of all me, since I was the heavy sleeper in the house.

The kitchen window was open, and I inhaled the sweet, clean air. It smelt of grass and magnolia blossoms. The French press was rinsed clean and resting in the dish drainer, someone had obviously used it, so I searched around for any left-over coffee grounds and found them in the mortar bowl, covered by a cloth with the pestle beside it, resting on the bench. The electric coffee grinder is too noisy to be used first thing in the morning, and I silently thanked the person who was there before me. I can't use the mortar and pestle without making a racket.

Coffee in hand, I made my way back to my room. A doorway from each of our bedrooms opened onto the back verandah which encircled the house. I stepped out of my bedroom onto the back deck. The deck overlooks the road leading into the property.

Max was sitting at the far end outside his bedroom with a cup of coffee in one hand and a cigarette in the other. The cigarette was an indication he had had another nightmare, a bad one. Max's nightmares always consisted of someone chasing him. The bogeyman, he told me once when I asked.

Sometimes I teased him with, 'The bogeyman chasing you again, Max?'

But not this morning.

He and Mum shared the same extreme stress indicator: the cigarette was a sure sign we needed to leave them alone until they expunged their demons and were ready to join the family.

I savoured my first cup of coffee, sitting watching the sun rise slowly over the horizon until it touched the trees with the first rays of its light.

A family of tawny frogmouths sat immobile, blending skilfully with the dark roughness of an ironbark tree.

The morning chorus started slowly. The first note, which was so pure it gave me goosebumps, was from a magpie, another replied with the same tune, and then the butcher birds joined in until the air was filled with birdsong. Noisy, joyful, and full of life.

I spent the first hour catching up on paperwork.

My cleaning business started, by chance, when I was fifteen. An elderly friend needed help after falling and breaking her arm. Mum offered her my services after school, and then life stepped in. The business found an energy of its own, and I had a ready-made job. All I needed to do was turn up.

Word of mouth spread like wildfire in our small community, and by the time I finished grade twelve, my business was thriving, and I stepped out of school into self-employment.

Except for Max sitting at his end of the verandah and looking miserable, the morning started like any other.

Mum and my two brothers, Sam and Max usually enjoyed a lie-in on Saturdays while I pottered around putting finishing touches to paperwork, checking supplies, sorting out appointments and creating a list of things needed for the coming week.

Glancing through my appointment book, it was clear I needed help; however, I was reluctant to expand the business. I liked being self-employed; I wasn't sure I wanted to have an employee that I would have to supervise. I sat for a while contemplating the pros and cons of employing someone and decided it was something I'd have to give some serious thought to and revisit.

Sam and Max worked our thousand-acre farm. It had once been part of a larger station owned by our family for generations. Mum, being an only child and with no one to help her, sold the station after my father left us. He walked out, leaving mum with eight-year-old Sam, six-year-old Max and pregnant with me.

There was a special bond between my brothers and Mum, one that had never included me. Don't get me wrong though – I am loved.

Max and Sam are the most loving and protective brothers anyone would want. Occasionally, it crossed my mind that it was my brothers who raised me. Mum was loving and kind but disconnected. She often drew into herself a little too far, and it was hard for me to reach her.

Sam and Max, ever sensitive to Mum, would take over my care and distract me until Mum returned from wherever she went. However, there were times when I felt they were too protective, especially when I wanted to attract the attention of a boy. Which, come to think of it, was why I was nineteen and without a boyfriend.

Mum's parents died four years apart before my brothers were born. My only living grandparent, my father's mother, lived in town; however, Mum refused to have anything to do with her. My brothers followed Mum's lead. Recently, I contacted her through my business, but so far, I hadn't told Mum or my brothers. It seemed best if I kept that little piece of information to myself. I wasn't sure what the fallout would be, and besides, I wanted to form my own opinion of her.

The thousand acres we farmed was freehold and on a separate title to the original station. Mum always said it was the only thing she could think to do at the time. Farming was all she knew, but she didn't want to run a large station by herself. By selling, she had the money to build a home and work the farm with the help of her uncle: Uncle Arthur who became the grandfather I never had.

Mum said she had been thinking of getting in touch with him when he arrived on her doorstep one day and told her he had come to help out. He was her mother's youngest brother – a bachelor, who Mum had only met a few times growing up but remembered him as a sweet, capable man. What she remembered the most about him was the sense of peace he always brought with him.

His memory, she told us, also conjured in her mind a picture of her father shaking his head in bewilderment every time Uncle Arthur left to visit temples in far off countries, such as India and the Himalayas. Sam and Max loved him on sight and followed him around, emulating his every move. Mum often said that his addition to the household was like a breath of fresh air.

He chose to live in a small cottage Mum built for him on the other side of the property, away from us and everyone else, in the bush with his four dogs for company.

As the boys grew, their roles in the farm increased until Mum decided she was happier keeping the books and pottering in the garden Uncle Arthur created, which was large enough to feed us all. Her hobbies included reading and going to coffee with her friends at least twice a week.

I had finished my morning chores and was enjoying a second cup of coffee when I saw a car slow on the road and turn into our long driveway.

I glanced in Max's direction, he had disappeared off the verandah, which I took as a good sign – he often used some of Uncle Arthur's relaxation techniques to chase away the bogeyman.

I looked down at my watch; eight o'clock was too early for unexpected visitors, and since our property was a little off the beaten track, I thought it most likely the occupants were lost.

If only they had been lost tourists.

Instead, two policemen were now sitting on our couch looking relaxed and at home while we were all on edge and looking uncomfortable.

Sam had pulled a T-shirt on over long cotton pyjamas pants; his hair was tousled and his face unwashed. He had no problem letting everyone know he disliked the rude interruption to his morning lie-in. He scowled at the visitors. Max was dressed in jeans and T-shirt and didn't appear to be fazed by the morning visitors. Any signs of his bad night had gone, and he appeared relaxed. He was a master of self-control, learnt at the knee of Uncle Arthur.

I had shrugged on a cotton dressing grown over my pyjamas before going out to meet the people who had disrupted our morning. When I discovered our visitors were police and not someone I could send on their way, like Max I changed into a pair of jeans and T-shirt.

The one obviously in charge introduced himself

as Detective Sergeant Neil Law. I stifled a grin and wondered if he had chosen his career based on his name. He was older than his companion, probably late twenties, like Max and Sam. He also had an edge to him that the constable did not. An air of authority or something more? I couldn't decide, but I wouldn't have wanted to cross him.

The other young man, Detective Constable James Drury, sat and watched us with hooded eyes. His bright-green eyes had been the first thing I noticed when I opened the door to see who our visitors were, before he scowled at me, and I scowled back. His hair was a darker brown than Sergeant Law's, and he was definitely the better looking.

Mum offered coffee, and when they refused, she made coffee for her and my brothers.

My coffee was still on the verandah, going cold.

After Mum served the coffee and seated herself, the sergeant said, 'A body has been found, and we have reason to believe it may be your husband, Mrs Kelly.' The sergeant paused, and I thought for a moment that he looked like a cat patiently watching his prey.

A tense silence filled the room – it seemed to go on and on.

I felt the silence needed filling. 'Oh, I read about that in the paper a couple of weeks ago.'

Everyone else seemed a bit stunned.

'What reason could you possibly have for thinking the body is my ex-husband?' asked Mum with a certain asperity and an emphasis on the 'ex'. She was dressed in loose-fitting bamboo lounge pants and a long tunic. Blond highlights covered the grey in her light-brown hair. She was tall, slim and elegant and didn't look as if she had just gotten out of bed. At fifty-two, her face showed little signs of aging. Her hands told a different story: wrinkled and rough, Mum called them her 'workers hands'.

'A wallet was found near the body, and it was sufficiently intact for the driver's licence to be legible,' replied Sergeant Law.

I glanced at my family and wished that my focus had not been on the two detectives. I hadn't seen my brother's or Mum's reactions. But now I wished I had. There was a stillness about them with which I was familiar. It spoke to me of closing ranks, knowledge and secrets.

'He left us many years ago. And my name is not "Kelly", I changed it back to my maiden name after my husband left. My name is "Ayres", as is my children's.'

'Can you tell me about the last time you saw him alive?' The sergeant's voice was low, calm.

'The day he left,' Mum's reply was terse, and she didn't elaborate.

'Have you kept in touch?'

'No.'

'Was there any particular reason he left?' asked Sergeant Law. His voice was soft, but his eyes reminded me of a cat lining up its next meal.

'Because I told him to.' Mum's tone indicated there was nothing more to be said.

A jolt of surprise swept through me. This was news to me. I had always been told 'the bastard left us, and good riddance'.

The constable must have registered my surprise, his green eyes swung to me; I attempted to mask my shock by scowling at him again. Our gazes held for a second before he returned to watching everyone with his eyes now narrowed.

With a long pause, Sergeant Law seemingly considered Mum's reply, and I had the impression he was giving her space to add something to her rather terse response.

The long pause became an awkward silence.

Sergeant Law cleared his throat. 'Anyway, if one of your children would be willing to provide DNA, I'm sure this matter can be settled, and we can at least confirm or deny that the body is your husband's.'

'Where did you find the body? And what makes you think it's my father. And how did this person die?' The questions tumbled out of me, and suddenly I found myself the focus of two sets of very sharp eyes.

'At the moment, all we can say is the body was found by campers in the vicinity of a neighbouring property, and our investigations are ongoing.'

I took this as police speak for 'none of your business and we'll ask the questions, thank you very much'. So, I thought, *well, up yours too, mate*, as Uncle Arthur would say.

'Our first task is to conclusively identify the body, so DNA is crucial.' Constable Drury swiftly seemed to find his voice, which I thought was smooth and rich like caramel. His eyes and voice added up to one sexy man. 'Once we know for sure, then we can give you more information.'

Max, who had started sipping his coffee, placed the cup on the table with a slight bump. Any sound from Max was unusual; he was very deliberate in his actions.

His calculated movement told me he had picked up on my interest in the constable's seductive voice. I glanced at him and saw him roll his eyes and give a barely perceptible shake of his head, which indicated that James Drury was off limits.

I raised my middle finger and ran it slowly along the side of my nose. (A rude trick I had learnt from my brothers.)

Max ignored me, and the constable appeared unaware of our interactions, but I saw the sergeant's lips twitch.

'Well, if it's him, we have no idea how he got there,' said Mum tartly. 'All we know is that he left. He was gone before Martha was born.' She indicated me with a nod.

'Martha Jane,' I interjected. 'I prefer, Jane.'

'That was twenty years ago.' Mum finished, as if I hadn't spoken. She too seemed oblivious to nuances.

'DNA is being recovered from the body, and we need to compare it with a close relative,' said the sergeant. He wasn't much older than his companion, but he had a stillness that gave him maturity.

I noticed answering questions was not one of the sergeant's stronger points.

'You have to tell us something.' I huffed. 'Stop being so bloody enigmatic. Or was the man murdered, is that what you're dancing around the mulberry bush about?' (Another one of Uncle Arthur's sayings.)

The sergeant's lips twitched again, or was it my imagination? Maybe he had a tic.

'We can't tell you anything more until we've investigated the matter further. We'd like to know if the ID found matches the DNA.'

'I'll do it,' offered Sam. 'What do I have to do?'

I zoned out as the detectives explained to Sam what was required. It suddenly occurred to me that if DNA confirmed the body to be my father's, then the narrative of my life had changed.

My father had left us, that had been part of my story my whole life. I hadn't missed not having a father. My brothers stepped into that role, and while I often wondered about the man who fathered me, I realised it was as an abstraction. Not something I truly cared about. I hadn't even been curious enough to ask about him. However, instead of rejecting us, as everyone thought, he may have lain dead and undiscovered in a gully on a neighbouring property.

*How unfair*, I thought. All these years and I thought

he had not deserved even thinking about. If it was him, how did he die, and why was he discarded like some animal carcass to be dumped and forgotten?

In one morning, my safe, ordered little world shifted.

After the detectives left, we sat in silence, and I looked with changed eyes at my brothers and Mum. Their silence was different to mine. I saw the voiceless communication between them and tried to make them include me. 'Is anyone going to tell me what's going on? Could it be him? Did Dad just up and leave us, or did you tell him to leave? Mum?'

Silence again, empty this time.

I felt a void open, and a sudden fear knifed through me. 'MUM?' I yelled. I could tell by her eyes that she had retreated to somewhere inside her head.

She stared at me blankly for a moment. 'It would explain why he never came back.' It was as if she were talking to herself, searching for an explanation. 'I always thought it had been too easy.'

'Too easy for what?'

'For him to leave us.' Max's voice was quiet, but there was something behind it that I had always sensed in him but couldn't articulate until now: a deep, fathomless pain.

'Max!' The warning in Mum's voice was unmistakeable.

'Jane won't leave it alone, Mum. You must know that? Anyway, if it's him or not, you can't shield her anymore. She's not a child.'

'Tell me!' I insisted. I knew there was *something* that I had always felt excluded from.

Sam was silent, which meant he agreed with Max.

A look passed between the three of them.

Suddenly Mum's shoulders slumped, and she gave a slight nod. For a moment, she rested her head in her hands, then she looked at me. 'Even if we tell you, you can't possibly know what it was really like.'

I looked at my brothers. 'Tell me.'

## Chapter Two

# Max

The hot sun was unbearable and Max felt its relentless rays burning his scalp. Perspiration plastered his hair into a damp sticky mess while rivulets of salty water slid down his face. His hat, knocked from his head by his father ten minutes ago, lay in the dirt several feet away. Sweat blinded his eyes, and his shirt and pants clung to his small frame, held there by the moisture bleeding from his body in an effort to keep it cool. He blinked rapidly to clear the sweat, but it seemed to drive the salt deeper into his eyes. He wanted to cry, but knew the moment he did, his father would tell him he was a baby. And that too would be punished.

The wire cutters were heavy and growing heavier with each passing moment. The cutters looked small in his father's hands, but Max could barely lift them, let alone hold them up long enough to cut the piece of wire from the post.

'He can't do it, he's only six years old!'

*Shut up, Sam.* Max silently pleaded. *Just shut up.* A small groan escaped his lips, and he hoped his father hadn't heard. If he couldn't cut the wire, then his father would punish Sam. He always punished Sam.

Max looked down at his puny hands and wished they were the size of this father's. Man size hands that could easily use the wire cutters. Large fists that could punch his father so hard he would never stand up again. The frisson of anger felt good. Better than fear or despair. It faded with Sam pleading with his father.

'I'll do it, Dad. Let me.'

'You. You're just as bad as he is. A pair of weaklings. No, I'm going to sit in the shade and have smoko. He's going to do it or you're going to know the reason why. And don't you help him, because I'll be watching.'

Tears welled up in Max's eyes and spilled over, mingling with sweat.

'Turn your head,' Sam softly cautioned. 'Don't let him see you cry.'

Max turned his head and surreptitiously wiped his eyes on the sleeve of his shirt.

'Have a rest,' whispered Sam. 'He'll be a little while. I'll have a look, see if you can attack it from another angle.'

Max dropped the wire cutters to the ground. Then he followed them down. His body was shaking with exhaustion, and his legs felt all jelly-like.

'Shit. Don't do that. It'll make him worse if they're dirty. Here, give them to me.' Sam scooped up the cutters and wiped the dirt off them with his shirt.

Max could feel his heart pounding, and his breaths came in gasps. He was so exhausted he wasn't sure his legs would hold him anymore. He wished he was back at the homestead with Mum making cakes. He loved helping her cook, and more than that, he loved eating the results.

'Look at this,' whispered Sam. 'He's been getting you to cut the thick side. There's a thin side.' Sam helped Max to his feet and used his shirt to wipe the sweat from his face. Then he grasped the cutters and positioned them over the thinner part of wire. The wire held the cutters in place against the post.

With Sam's help, Max gripped the cutters with both hands, and using his body as leverage, he pushed against the handle. The wire parted with a satisfying *thwack*.

Relief flowed through Max's body. He had done it. Sam was safe.

And then he saw his father coming towards them, his eyes full of hate, tight-lipped and radiating anger.

Fear and rage flared within Max in equal measure, and he stepped in front of Sam and yelled, 'You leave him alone, you leave him alone.'

## Chapter Three

# Jane

We were all so intent on Max, we jumped when Uncle Arthur spoke.

'I think that's enough for now.' The doorway framed him – an old man, tall and sinewy with gentle brown eyes that spoke of strength and endurance. 'To Max,' he said, and four Kelpies slipped in from behind and went to Max.

One sat at his feet, another on his lap, and the other two went either side of him. Max slipped his arms around them all; he seemed to be gaining comfort from their furry bodies.

I wiped away the tears cascading down my face, but I couldn't erase the pain in my heart or the horror that I felt.

'C'mon, on your feet. You all need to walk.'

We followed Uncle Arthur meekly, and he led us into the cool of the forest.

Large gums, with their tallest branches swaying in the fresh, soft breeze, surrounded us. A crow cawed loudly in the distance. Two butterflies danced above the high grass. Peace eased its way into my body, and I saw it reflected in the faces of my family.

Uncle Arthur said, 'Free,' and the dogs, given permission to roam at will, tore off into the bush. 'Hopefully, they'll bring me back a rabbit for dinner.' He turned to me then, looking deeply into my eyes.

I don't know how long I looked into his eyes, but for the first time, I felt I was truly seeing him, and he knew it. If it hadn't been Uncle Arthur, I think I would have been frightened, and I couldn't have said why.

'You'll hear more, no doubt, in the coming weeks or months ... however long it takes them to tell their stories. And always remember that you can't fix this, and don't become angry for their benefit or your own. They've hidden their pain to give you the childhood they didn't have, so don't waste it on self-pity, resentment, or righteous anger. Your job here is simply to listen … and maybe in time, you'll understand.'

I nodded, but only because he obviously expected me too, and I think he knew that.

'Stay close to nature … it will bring you peace. Be aware of your own energy, and do your best not to be affected by the energies around you. Call it what you will, but we're all connected by the same thing. Don't let this knowledge colour the rest of your life.'

He then wandered off and I followed, understanding the words in my mind but feeling confused by them as well.

We followed him down to the river. At its shallowest part, a pool of cold water lay sheltered by the shadows of the trees. We all stripped down to our undies and slid, with many gasps, into its refreshing depths.

Suddenly, Max splashed me. I looked up. He grinned, and the fight was on. We splashed and laughed our way back to each other.

It was only afterwards that I realised I had been unable to meet his eyes, afraid of what might show on my face. He wouldn't want pity.

Uncle Arthur came back to the house with us, and

we shared a large breakfast, with hot coffee, bacon, eggs, and lots of thick toast made from Mum's home-made bread.

The dogs returned eventually, with two rabbits, and Uncle Arthur took that as his cue to leave us.

Much later, I said to Mum, 'It's like he delivered a sermon, said a prayer and baptised us.'

'Not "like", love. He did. That man saved us. The boys and me.' She didn't elaborate, and she didn't need to. Uncle Arthur was special in ways that, had someone asked, I wouldn't have been able to define; a peace flowed through him that touched all our lives.

Any sense of well-being I felt allowed me a peaceful night's sleep, but with the coming of Sunday morning, I opened my eyes to a new reality. One where I felt I had been spawned by the devil.

The sun shone under the blinds in my bedroom. I could tell it was late, but I didn't want to get out of bed. The ceiling of my bedroom had never been more interesting. Cobwebs clung to the corners of the room; their makers were no longer visible. Hidden somewhere, I supposed. This morning, I too wanted to hide.

A sudden feeling of shame engulfed me. My brothers had lived it, and I wanted to hide merely from the knowledge of my dad's cruelty.

My world had tilted, and it would never be the same. I hadn't seen my brothers' pain, nor Mum's. *Had I been blind, naïve, selfish?* Perhaps I had been all those things, but my brothers and Mum had taken great care to hide their pain from me. They shielded me and coddled me and pretended all was well in our world. Had it all been a lie? What else was a lie? That Dad had left us?

If the body in the gully was his, how did it get there? No doubt, the police were asking themselves the same question. And with that thought, a whole new feeling of horror awoke in me. Had they killed him? Who? Sam was eight and Max six. So, I figured it must have happened not long after that appalling story Max told yesterday.

They couldn't have killed him. *Mum? Nah, not possible. How was she going to throw a man into a gully? Roll him? Push him? She could have had help. Uncle Arthur?* I thought he had come later. Was I mistaken about that?

I couldn't picture anyone in my family killing someone, but then I hadn't been aware of the abuse they had suffered.

25

It could have been someone else …

What did I know of his life? I had taken my cues from Mum and my brothers. They were relieved and grateful he had gone, and so I had been also.

Dad had been born and raised in this area; someone must know something about him.

Memories rose unbidden and floated across the front of my mind.

'I knew your father. He was a good man.' I remembered the man's face for a second. I hadn't known him but knew instinctively there was something he was leaving unsaid.

'Good men don't leave their families,' I had retorted, and he shuffled off.

'Your brothers seem sad,' a classmate said when I was six years old.

'No, they're not, don't be silly.'

I had an answer for everyone.

She had seen, so why hadn't I?

'I worked with your dad for a time. Had a hell of a temper.' I knew this man but couldn't put a name to him.

Tomorrow, my first client was going to be my estranged grandmother. Not that I expected anything from her. Our first meeting had been awkward, made more awkward by her insisting I call her Mrs Kelly.

'Oh, I thought …' I had stammered.

Her abruptness surprised me. 'You're not calling me "grandma" or anything like that. This is the first time we've met; (*whose fault was that,* I thought) relationships are more than blood. Though I must say you do remind me of Lincoln (I almost said, "who's that", then I remembered that was Dad's name); so does the second boy … What's his name?'

'Max.'

'Yeah, well, the eldest one doesn't look like Lincoln at all.'

'Well, there is my mother's side of the family. He has more than one set of DNA.'

Her eyes narrowed, and a sneer briefly twisted her lips. She then actually snorted!

After meeting her, I felt sorry for the man who had been her son and my dad.

I was having trouble even saying 'Dad' in my head. 'Sperm donor' was the correct term. My brothers had been the father-figures in my life.

The water pump kicked in; someone had turned a tap on. A cupboard door opened. I heard the rattle of crockery and the door being shut. Mum was up. Only Mum made that much noise. Sam and Max could cook themselves breakfast without rattling a pan.

I closed my eyes and swore silently under my breath. *Why don't I have my own place, where if I don't want to face anyone then I don't have to.*

In the end, my bladder forced me out of bed and into the bathroom.

The face looking back at me in the mirror looked the same as ever. Blue eyes and dark-brown hair, a feature I shared with Max and inherited from 'Lincoln'. Sam inherited Mum's light-brown hair and soft-brown eyes. Hence Grandmother Kelly's remark about Sam. *Silly woman*, I thought, suddenly grumpy with her narrow view and stupid insinuations.

I was glad I could take my time and that I didn't have to share a bathroom. I could thank Mum for that. She designed the house so that we all had our own retreats within the house. It was probably why we were all still living together.

Not ready, but I knew I couldn't delay any longer, I made my way to the kitchen.

Uncle Arthur sat at the kitchen table, coffee cup in hand, watching Mum cook breakfast. 'Hey, Martha,

I wanted some company moving the cattle today. Do you want to join me? Blow the cobwebs away?'

He was the only person who called me Martha. I didn't usually ignore being called Martha, but I let it pass – bigger things were on my mind. 'Sure, why not? You coming, Mum?'

She nodded and concentrated on her cooking.

We moved our three hundred head of cattle through a rotational grazing system. Smaller paddocks and daily moving meant there was no need for artificial fertilizers; it also increased the quality of the soil, which in turn produced better-quality grass. An added bonus was that with so much contact, the cattle were calmer when we needed to handle them, and it gave us the chance to check the cows that were due to calve and any other problems they might be having. Uncle Arthur's dogs did the majority of the work; a whistle or soft word directed them to where he wanted them to go.

In nature, I relaxed and enjoyed the smell and calm energy of the cattle, so I was happy to tag along.

It occurred to me that that was how Uncle Arthur came to be passing the house yesterday when the detectives were here. It was then I realised that some small part of me thought of him as psychic, turning up when he did as if he knew we needed him.

'Where's Sam and Max?' I asked.

'Gone to see if they can find the gully where the body was found,' Mum replied.

'Oh,' was the only reply I could manage, but I wished they had taken me with them. But then they left me out of a lot of things.

## Chapter Four

# Sam

Sam gazed down into the steep ravine. 'How the bloody hell was he found?'

If not for the obvious signs of disturbance that had been needed to retrieve the body, the bush was thick. Thick enough to obscure the bottom of the gully.

It had, after all, kept its secret for twenty years.

*What had occurred to make anyone look down there?* Sam wondered. Unlike Jane, he hadn't heard the news about a body being discovered, and the detectives hadn't explained anything, really.

'Beats me,' was all Max said in reply.

'Do you think it's him?' asked Sam.

'I hope so,' Max said emphatically. 'A part of me was always worried the bastard would return. Anyway, we'll find out when we get the DNA results.'

'Will we?'

Max glanced at Sam. 'Don't even go there, mate. We might have different colouring, but we do look alike. He only said that to hurt you and to justify his viciousness.'

'Yeah, but over and over, he said I wasn't his kid. Maybe it's true,' Sam replied.

'And maybe it's not. Anyway, Mum never turned a hair when you volunteered your DNA.'

'Well, if our DNAs match, then it's him, and even if they don't match, it could still be him.'

'If they don't match, and he's not your father, then think yourself bloody lucky that you don't have his genetics running around inside of you. If yours don't match, I'm not getting it done, it's the last thing that I want confirmed. To be that mongrel's son.'

Sam looked at his brother; he could feel anxiety building inside of him and took several deep, calming breaths before asking, 'How much are you going to tell Jane?'

Max returned his gaze, with calmer eyes. 'Don't worry. Not too much, certainly not all of it, but as much as she needs to know without telling her too much. To be honest, I think I threw a spanner into Jane's safe little world yesterday.' His grin softened his words.

Sam knew they weren't coming from an intent to wound.

Max paused for a moment then said, 'I'm not telling her anything about you, mate. Your story is yours to tell.'

Sam nodded and turned towards the motorbikes. 'Best we get back. Uncle Arthur will be along to move the cattle soon.'

'Believe me, he's already there, and no doubt, he's dragging Mum and Jane along with him. Knowing him, he'll be wanting to get them out into nature. That's his answer to everything stressful.'

A smile hovered at the corner of Sam's mouth, and he nodded, glad of Max's calm, no nonsense approach to life.

## Chapter Five

# Jane

I arrived at 'Mrs Kelly's' place on Monday, at the appointed time, eight o'clock, and the door opened as I reached it. She had obviously been looking out for me.

Stepping through the door, I placed the accoutrements of my trade on the floor. I turned to her with an intake of breath.

'Before you start,' she began. 'And I don't mean the cleaning …'

'Oh.' I let out the breath with a *whoosh*.

The gleam in her eyes and the hands on her hips told me she was ready to fight.

'Yes, the police came, and no, I'm not going to give my DNA, and no, I don't care if it's him or not. I lost him a long time ago, and I mourned him then. It's over for me, and I don't wish to discuss it.' Her face was flushed and her lips razor-thin. Despite her words, she looked like she had been crying and would start again at any minute.

Everything I had been going to say and ask vanished from my mind. 'Well, if you find out anything, could you share it with us ... please. I just wanted to know what he was like?'

She stared at me for a long moment, so much so that I was beginning to think that maybe she had had a stroke and couldn't understand what I was saying.

'I suggest, young lady, that there are some things best left alone. Don't do my bedroom today. I'm going to have a lie down.'

I would have liked to yell at her and tell her how selfish she was, but the thought occurred to me that she wasn't acting from selfishness, just some deep, unspoken pain.

Was there anyone's life that wasn't full of pain once 'Lincoln' touched it?

*

My next three clients all worked during the day, so I was alone with my thoughts as I cleaned their homes.

My head was full of Mrs Kelly's grief-stricken face. Her words had been harsh, but her body language told another story, and one I hoped that in time, and with a lot of patience on my part, she would share with me. The more I found out about the man who fathered me, the more despondent I became. Who was this man? How did he get to be part of my mum's life? He had certainly not brought joy to the lives he touched.

Usually, I made my lunch and ate it in the park under a large, shady tree. But today, I wanted people around me, someone and something else to think about, so I chose a café in town that made the best coffee, sandwiches and cakes. I sat in a corner and thought that I would do some people-watching while I ate my lunch.

The first person to sit down at my table was Detective Sergeant Law. 'Mind if I sit,' he asked as he was already in the process of sitting.

'And if I said no?' I responded.

'Oh well.' He shrugged sheepishly and grinned. He was dressed more casually today: blue jeans, T-shirt and loafers. Light-blue eyes twinkled at me. A lock of brown hair fell across his eyes, and he flicked it away.

He seemed not to notice, and I thought that it was a regular occurrence that had become a habit.

I smiled back at him. 'Sorry, I'm in a bit of a mood. I saw Mrs Kelly ... I mean, my grandmother today and ...'

'Say no more. We spoke to her also, and she sent us away with a flea in our ear.'

I laughed. 'You sound like my Uncle Arthur; he has all those old sayings tucked away that he trots out at the appropriate moments. They always seem so apt.' I bit my lip before I then asked, 'Do you have any news?'

He shook his head; his eyes had sharpened, and I knew in that instant that this man was nobody's fool.

He was also very attractive, now that I had had a second look. He didn't wear a wedding ring, but I knew that meant nothing. I may not have had a proper boyfriend, but I had enough friends who had been burnt, and then there were my two brothers who had lectured me on the ways of some men.

'Your brother is going to get DNA tested today, isn't he?'

'Do you always answer a question with a question?' I countered.

The waitress placed my order in front of me.

Sergeant Law's eyes twinkled at me again. 'We'll meet again after we get the results.' Nonchalantly, he rose from the seat and wandered off.

Why had he even bothered to sit and talk with me? He asked for nothing and gave nothing. *Strange man. Cute but odd.*

Two sips of coffee later and a man I didn't know slipped into the seat the sergeant had just left. He regarded me with sly eyes; however, his tone was friendly, almost ingratiating. 'I worked with your father when he was a young man. He was a very hard worker, a good man. It's a shame what's happened to him.'

I took another sip of my coffee. The image of a small, frightened Max slipped into my head and I stared, with unfriendly eyes at the stranger. 'What did happen to him?' I asked. My tone was frosty.

The man blinked. 'Well, they found his body, didn't they?' His tone also changed.

'No, they found *a* body. No one knows who it is?'

He regarded me with colder eyes. 'Hmmph,' was all he said before he too left.

I checked the top of my head and all around for any sign that may have said: *all welcome, sit down and annoy me while I'm trying to grab a bite to eat.*

Typical of small and not-so-small towns – everyone knew everyone else's business and had an opinion. His opinion of Lincoln was much higher than it had any right to be, but then I supposed we judged people on how they treated us, not how they treated others. I could ask a hundred people about him, and I would get as many different answers as possible.

I picked up my sandwich to take a bite and caught the eye of a man I hadn't seen since we were in high school. Ant Thompson was sitting three tables away, and a waitress was taking his order. He was the son of Mum's oldest friend, Fletcher Thompson, who was our neighbour.

Four years older than me, Ant and I met at high school and quickly became inseparable. I felt such a strong bond with him, I thought I had found the other half of myself. We both had been devastated when his parents abruptly sent him off to a distant boarding school. I thought my heart would never recover.

It did, but all the same, it started hammering away at the sight of him now.

Ant waved and indicated to the waitress that he would join me at my table.

I rose as he approached, and without thinking, we stepped into each other's arms.

I was home.

Ant had changed from the awkward youth I had known and loved into a man who was comfortable in his own skin. Any sign of the country boy I knew was gone. He looked as if he was from the city, dressed in jeans and a Khaki Henley shirt. Ant's reddish-blond hair had darkened to brown with red highlights, and his serious grey eyes softened and sparkled at me.

'I was hoping I would see you. Dad told me not to intrude on your family. Your mum rang and filled him in on what was going on … you know, the body and all that.'

'Rubbish,' I said. 'As if you would be intruding, you're like family to me.'

In acknowledgment, he gave me another hug and a kiss on the forehead.

We sat alongside one another, holding hands and staring into each other's eyes. It was a bit cliched, I know, but it was as if we wanted to drink in the other in case they disappeared again. Well, I know I did, and he certainly appeared to feel the same. He didn't seem to be able to take his eyes off me, and he held my hand as if it were a lifeline.

In the years since I had last seen him, I thought that what I felt at thirteen had been the intensity of first love, or first infatuation. Now, I wasn't so sure. Those same feelings came surging back.

'Is it really your dad that they found? At least, that's what your mum told my dad ... and it's of course what the gossips are saying.'

I shrugged. I didn't want to talk to Ant about Lincoln. 'We don't know. Sam's getting a DNA sample done today for comparison.' I paused. 'Forget about all that. What are you doing here? What have you been doing? I hear about you from time to time when Mum catches up with your mum, but that doesn't seem to happen very often.'

A puzzled look flitted across his face. He shook his head as if to chase a fly away.

'Ah, well ... let's see. I'm in my third year of medicine at Sydney uni. Loving it.' A serious change swept across his face and his eyes darkened. 'I'm here because Mum was admitted to hospital.' He held my hand tighter. 'And now that I'm here, I think it's more emotional than physical.'

'Look at you,' I teased. 'Already sounding like a doctor.'

We laughed but the worry never quite left his face.

'Is she going to be all right?' I asked as I gently rubbed his shoulder.

'Sure. She's getting out of hospital tomorrow.' He paused, then finished with, 'She's fine.'

I could tell there was more that he wanted to say, but Ant's order arrived, and the waitress' presence stopped our chat. The moment passed, and we picked at our food and sipped our drinks.

'Mum tells me you're cleaning houses for a living.'

'Don't sound so … so … snobbish,' I retorted. 'Since when did you become a snob?'

He chuckled. 'Got you,' he said softly.

I punched his arm lightly. 'Prick … Actually, I like having my own business. I like the responsibility and the freedom. I choose who I work for and what I'm prepared to do.'

'Are you seeing anyone?' he asked.

'No. My brothers are still frightening everyone away.' I laughed, before continuing, 'No, that's not true … I just haven't found anyone I'm really keen on, and I'm not interested in hook-ups or anything casual. My brothers might kill me if I did.' And I was only half-joking.

'What about you? Anyone?'

Ant shook his head. 'No. Not really,' he said hesitantly.

'What does that mean? Either you are or you aren't.'

A red spot appeared between his eyebrows.

I smiled inwardly. Still the same old Ant, couldn't tell a lie if he tried. That red spot was his tell. A kernel of disappointment budded somewhere in the middle of my chest, and I took a deep breath to try to dislodge it. Of course, he had someone. He was attractive, kind, intelligent and funny. He probably had a lot of women after him.

'We're off at the moment.' He then said slowly, 'That's the problem, we spend more time off than on. It's like an addiction. We fight when we're together, and when we're apart, we're miserable. It's a roller-coaster that I've been trying to get off.' He reached out tentatively and gently stroked my hand.

It was a whisper touch that ignited something inside of me. My insides felt as if they were melting.

'I've just realised that I want a lover who is also a friend, but at the moment, it just doesn't seem possible,' he muttered, seemingly more to himself than to me.

Across the table, our fingers intwined and we held on: me in wordless sympathy, knowing that there could be nothing between us until he was truly free, and he, well … he just looked miserable, and I wondered what he was thinking.

His jaw tightened, and he released a puff of breath through his nose. He then raised my hand to his lips and kissed my fingers lightly before releasing them. 'Can I see you tomorrow. Here, for lunch again.' His voice was louder, confident again.

'If it's not too hot, I eat in the park. I only came here to distract myself. Give me your phone number, and I'll text you where I'm going to be tomorrow.'

Once outside, we stood in awkward silence by the side of my car. He looked as uncomfortable as I felt. Had he already changed his mind about seeing me tomorrow. There was so much I wanted to say, and eventually I managed, 'Well, it was lovely to see you again.'

He grinned down at me. 'So polite, Miss Ayres,' he teased.

'Shut up,' I muttered.

'Ah … um … one thing before you go.' His frown had deepened, and I thought, *he's changed his mind, he doesn't want to meet tomorrow.* Instead, he said something that astounded me. 'You said our mum's only catch up occasionally, but they don't … They're good friends. They've been close for a very long time, as long as I can remember.'

'What?'

'I know. It's odd. Look, don't tell your mum you've seen me.'

I felt baffled by his request. Generally, I told Mum everything. Well maybe not *everything*. But I saw no reason to keep this from her; in fact, I was so excited after seeing him again that I couldn't wait to tell her.

He must has seen the confusion cross my face. 'Just for now.' His eyes pleaded, though he clearly could see that I still wasn't convinced. 'I just don't know why your mum would pretend she wasn't friends with my mum. It doesn't make sense.' He shook his head. 'Think about it then,' he said before gathering me into his arms and kissing me lightly on the forehead.

All I could do was nod as he opened the door and saw me safely seated in my car.


Shirley was my last client of the day. I usually left her for last so we could have a cup of tea and a long chat if we wanted. She was the closest thing to a grandmother that I had. Our age difference didn't bother either of us.

Outside the family, she was probably my best friend. I had friends my own age, but somehow growing up in a family surrounded by people so much older than me, I had somehow skipped the partying that my friends seemed to love so much.

The truth was, I had been trying my best to carry on as normal, but my world had tilted, and I wasn't sure it would ever right itself.

For ten minutes, I sat in the car outside of Shirley's house and wondered what I was going to say to her. She would know something was wrong. Hers had been the first house I cleaned; it was Shirley who had kickstarted my career as a cleaner.

Her family had been in the district as long as mine, which was as long as Europeans had settled in the area. I was there to clean her house, but she had long been my confidante. However, I couldn't betray the secrets that my brothers and Mum had held onto for so long. I included Mum because after leaving Ant, I made a rather long detour past the hospital, and I was more than puzzled to find Mum's car in the parking lot. *Is she visiting Ant's mother, or someone else? Why does she pretend an acquaintance with someone when they're actually good friends?*

Maybe I wouldn't say anything to Mum about meeting up with Ant. And what had made Ant even suggest that I say nothing?

I wasn't sure of anything anymore, but while it seemed to me that if I said anything, I would be being disloyal to my family, I also knew that telling Shirley anything would be like going to the confessional.

What would I say to her, though? Would she know anything about Lincoln? Unlike some of my clients who were really nosy, she never mentioned him; our talks were only about her family, and news of interest. She never pried and would only talk to me about my family when I introduced them as a subject for discussion. Still, if I was going to confide in anyone, it would be Shirley. And I did need to debrief to someone who wasn't family.

Still unsure what I was going to say to her, I tentatively knocked on Shirley's door, which opened almost immediately.

'I thought you were going to sit out there all day,' she announced. She had obviously been watching my struggle from her window. 'Come in. I'll put the kettle on. I'm glad you're here,' she continued as I followed her into the house. 'One of the doors to my kitchen cabinet has come off its hinges, and my knees don't bend as well as they used to. I've made some scones, and I'll make a nice cup of tea while you put the door back on its hinges, and then if you want to, you can tell me why you were sitting out there looking like you didn't want to come in.'

I followed her voice down the corridor. She lived in an old Queenslander and had done so, from what I could gather, ever since she was first married.

Her voice drifted back to me. 'Though I think I know at least part of it ... The gossips have already been on the phone to me.'

We stood in her kitchen, and Shirley showed me the door and its loose hinge, then she directed me to her tool cupboard. I rummaged around until I found a screwdriver and some screws.

While I restored the door to its rightful position, Shirley set about preparing afternoon tea, and telling me in her low, calming voice how her latest great-grand-child had been born with a hare lip and cleft palate and that she was glad it had happened in this day and age because in her day the surgery to fix these conditions often left terrible scars.

My nerves subsided as I worked; I had sat in Shirley's

kitchen many times, and a sense of familiarity and comfort settled within me.

When I finished with the door, I washed my hands and took a seat at the kitchen table. The scones looked and smelt delicious. As usual, Shirley had set a formal table. There were no teabags in Shirley's home, and mugs were not used to drink tea. And while hooking a finger through the handle of a vintage teacup was near-impossible, the art of it, according to Shirley, was to use the thumb and index finger to hold the top of the handle while the middle finger supported the bottom. Believe me, it took practise.

While I enjoyed Shirley's way of doing things, I preferred the more casual style of home.

Two cups of hot tea and two delicious home-made scones with loads of strawberry jam and cream later, we sat in companionable silence.

Shirley's silence and her quiet sipping of her tea helped me slip into a state of deep relaxation. I felt the pressure of unanswered questions slip away. Here I was safe, and for the first time, I was aware of an undercurrent of tension that existed in my own home. *Why hadn't I been aware of it before? Had it always been there?*

'Do the police really believe that the body they found could be your father?' Shirley's voice interrupted by reverie and gave me a place to start.

'Mm. They found some sort of identification with the body, so they do think it's him, but they still want definitive proof, so Sam's going in today to get DNA tested. Well …' I glanced at my watch; he should have had it done by now. 'I don't know how long it's going to take, none of us thought to ask. I think we were all a bit shocked.' I paused, then with tears in my eyes and a heaviness in the pit of my stomach, I told her some of Max's story.

She pulled a clean handkerchief from her pocket and passed it across to me. Tissues were not part of Shirley's grocery list. 'Hmm. That, my dear, is unfortunately a common story. I believe that generally, your father was well liked and respected in the community. In my day, they were called "street angels and home devils".' She sat in quiet reflection; her thoughts had obviously taken a different road.

I sat watching different and conflicting emotions play across her face. The telling of Max's tale had produced a tempest within, and I took deep breaths and released them slowly, hoping to allay the storm gathering inside me. A part of me wanted to scream and yell, but that was not the way my family handled our emotions.

Shirley inhaled and exhaled sharply. 'I know how difficult it is to live with someone who pretends one thing to the world and is totally different at home. John's weapons were mainly words, but a man who has access to a woman's body has other ways to inflict harm.' She paused. 'I know you won't repeat this, and I've never told another soul.' She pressed her lips together as if to hold back the words, hesitated briefly, then she shook her head as if saying 'no'. And then with a look of determination on her face, she carried on, 'We were lying in bed one night. We had probably been married twenty years by then. I was reading an article in the Reader's Digest about a study that had been done that discovered a significant number of men would rape a woman if they knew they could get away with it. I asked John if he would rape someone if he could be sure he wouldn't be punished.' She paused again. Swallowed. Tears glistened in her eyes. 'He of course answered in the affirmative, but what I suddenly realised was that he had been getting away with it for years. Back then, it wasn't considered rape if one was married.'

Silence. Heavy and painful. I had no idea what to say.

'What was worse, I stayed,' she whispered. 'For the first time, I saw him clearly, and I finally understood why my sense of worth had all but left me.'

'I'm so sorry,' I replied softly.

She nodded, pulled another handkerchief from a different pocket, wiped her eyes and blew her nose. 'What do you know of your father?' she asked.

'Nothing really, except that he left us. Mum raised me and my brothers and ran the farm. She doesn't talk about him and neither do my brothers. I asked about him when I was younger but soon learnt he wasn't a topic anyone wanted to discuss. And to be honest, I haven't missed having a father. My brothers have more than filled that role. They took me to school, helped with my homework, played with me and allowed me to follow them around. I can honestly say I've had a happy childhood.'

'And your brothers, it seems, did not.'

Shirley's insight startled me. She was right. I had never thought about Sam and Max having anything different to me. After all, they shared my life. But they hadn't, and I felt stupid for not realising it. They had nine and seven years respectively that hadn't included me.

'I know you want answers,' Shirley continued, 'but

your family will not tell you the worst of what happened, only what they are prepared to share, so I want you to be sure that you think about this more carefully before you go much further. I knew your father when he was a boy, and by all accounts, he grew into a fine man, but ...' A look that I could not interpret passed across her face. Then her lips came together suddenly, and she sat quietly and stared out the window. She poured us both another cup of tea, and we sat with the only sound: us sipping our tea.

I waited and watched as Shirley clearly struggled with whatever was going through her mind.

'A friend of mine, a nurse ...' Shirley didn't look at me as she spoke, she seemed to be lost in a memory that she had dredged up from the depths of her mind. 'Told me about a young child who was admitted to hospital with terrible injuries to his whole body. His father, by all accounts a very well-respected member of the community, had strung him up on a barbwire fence as punishment for something his brother had done.'

Horrified at Shirley's story, I stared at her aghast. I couldn't see the relevance to my father or my family. 'Is this your way of saying that people aren't always what they seem?' I asked.

Shirley startled. 'What? Oh! Yes, of course. Now, my dear, you must go home. We have spoken for too long, and the house cleaning can wait. I'm the only one rattling around in it, so it doesn't get very dirty. You can slot me in for another day. Text me a time and date.'

Shirley may have been old-fashioned in her habits, but she was up to date with technology.

'Sure,' I replied as I carried the crockery and cutlery to the sink.

'Leave them, it won't take me a minute to clean everything.' She placed her hands on my shoulder and turned me to face her. 'Tread carefully. Your family loves you very much. But it's their feelings and their pain that you will trample on. I'm sure this matter will sort itself out eventually. And if it is your father, well good riddance to bad rubbish, is all I can say.'

I grinned at her. Like Uncle Arthur, she had an idiom for every occasion. I couldn't help but think that this one was extremely appropriate.

I felt calmer on the drive home. Shirley had not provided me with any answers, but she had sat with me and let me talk about my feelings of confusion when faced with a dead father left to rot in a bush grave versus a deserting bastard who didn't give a toss about his family.

And my family's strange reactions. That was the most upsetting thing of all.

Shirley's horror story of the abused child floated through my mind, and I tried to push it down, but it kept drifting back up.

Then with it came an image of a scarred back.

Slamming my foot on the brake, I pulled to the side of the road.

Sam's back was scarred. From being thrown from a horse onto a barbwire fence, he had told me.

## Chapter Six

# Kate

Kate's eyes roamed over her sleeping friend. Remnants of Nicole Thompson's beauty lingered in her red hair, which was once fiery but had dimmed with age and stress. Her skin was still soft and clear, which Kate's mother would have termed 'peaches and cream', but no longer firm. Long lashes fanned her cheeks, concealing brown eyes that had, in the past, radiated kindness and joy but now depicted anxiety more often.

Worry had etched itself into Nicole's face. Even in sleep, she couldn't let the fear go, and it seemed to saturate her whole body, made visible to Kate by her clenched hands.

Gently, Kate lifted one of her friend's hands, massaged it open and held it between her own, trying to impart her love, support and remorse through her touch.

When Kate first met Nicole at a party Fletcher had held to introduce her to his friends and family, she thought Nicole was the most innocent person she had ever encountered.

When she mentioned this to Fletcher, his laconic reply was, 'Yeah, well. Her father and mother think they're living in the Victorian era. Eight kids themselves, not sure they've worked out how that happened yet either. We have a bloody chaperone wherever we go. I'm barely allowed to hold her hand, without him scowling at me.' He indicated a man standing not far away, who was indeed scowling.

Kate laughed. 'She's perfect for you,' she had whispered to Fletcher, her best friend.

Fletcher had been in her life from early childhood. Their parents' stations had bordered each other, and they gravitated towards one another, drawn by a bond that remained unbreakable even to this day.

In the deepest part of her, Kate wished that she and Fletch had been more to each other. Unacknowledged to anyone but herself, she wished she had married him. Wished they had both settled for a marriage based on friendship instead of passion.

A gentle smile floated across Kate's face as she remembered the day she asked him to teach her to kiss. They used to meet at the river dividing their properties. After a swim, they shared the food they brought and talked about … what? She could no longer remember, but Kate did remember saying, 'I want to learn to kiss. All the girls at school are talking about the boys they've kissed, and I have no idea how. Will you teach me?' She then had added, 'You do know how, don't you?'

Fletcher, forever cool, under pressure had nonchalantly shrugged. 'Of course, I know how … Why, only this morning I kissed Flora … just before I milked her. Bit hairy but quite a kisser.' He chuckled.

And she had laughed with him. 'Idiot.'

'Don't you think that when the time comes, you'll know how?' he asked.

'What if I don't,' she retorted. 'What if I find someone I really, really want to kiss and then when I do, he goes "What a dud" … or whatever it is you boys says to each other. Have you kissed anyone?'

'Yeah, and she went "what a dud".'

When they had finished laughing, he looked at Kate intently. 'Seriously, K, no offense … but I can't kiss you, it would be like kissing one of my mates from school. That's just weird and … well … weird.'

Kate kneeled in front of him and pushed him in the chest. 'I'm not one of your mates from school. I'm not a boy. And I'm certainly not going to tell anyone. Anyway, we go to different schools, so who's going to know?'

And through laughter, derision, and sheer awkwardness, they joined lips, and both pulled away immediately before they cried, 'No. No more, we can't do it.'

Though sometimes, she thought he agreed so that he could learn as well. It wasn't as if either of them had much of a chance to practise on anyone else.

Even at sixteen, they both knew that there was no passion between them, only an abiding friendship.

Kate now looked up as Fletcher silently entered the room, a coffee in each hand. He passed one to her, and she gratefully took a sip and nodded her appreciation.

'You okay,' he asked softly.

'Yeah. Same old, same old. How could I have been so blind?'

'You gotta let it go, K. You've been beating yourself up for over twenty years, and what good has it done? Hasn't changed anything, has it?

Kate shook her head. 'No,' she said, almost inaudibly.

'I love you, K.'

'Thank you. I know. Me too, always.'

They sat in silence, gazing at the woman whose life had been so negatively impacted by their own lives.

Where had it all gone so wrong? How could she have been so blind?

Because he had made sure she was. He treated her like a queen, and behind her back, Lincoln was ... something she could never have imagined in her wildest dreams.

Kate remembered the day Lincoln entered her life. He wasn't handsome, but he was magnetic, with dark hair, blue eyes and a smile so wide it seemed like his whole face was smiling. He was Fletcher's friend first, someone he had known at school, not friends exactly but someone he had had the occasional drink with. They moved in circles that overlapped each other. And Lincoln Kelly was regarded as one of the 'good guys'.

And when he finally kissed her, she thought her whole body had been set alight. And it had been, with desire.

Nicole stirred, slipped her hand out of Kate's grasp and rubbed her hand across her forehead. Her eyes opened and slowly swept the room. She smiled and moved her tongue around dry lips. 'So good to see you two. I'm so thirsty.' Her voice sounded gravelly.

Fletcher was quick to pour the water and then assist Nicole to a sitting position, helping her to bring the cup to her lips.

Tears pricked Kate's eyes; gratitude flowed through her body.

She was comforted by the fact that Nicole and Fletcher's love seemed to have remained unbroken, dimmed a little by adversity in the Lincoln years, but it seemed to her that hardship had bound them together stronger than superglue.

Fletcher plumped her pillows while Nicole used the bathroom, and when she returned to bed, he fussed over her until she finally pushed him away with a smile.

'I'm fine, love. I do feel better, and I'm so sorry I over-reacted … as usual.' She gave a self-deprecating smile.

'It gave us all a shock,' said Kate. 'All these years, the boys and I have dreaded the thought that one day he would return. We never imagined he could be dead.'

'I know,' Nicole said softly. 'It's unthinkable, really.' She reached out and grasped Fletcher's hand. 'But we're glad, aren't we, love?'

Fletcher gave Nicole's hand a quick squeeze, released it and sat back in his chair, arms folded tight against his body. 'You might be,' he said with tension in his voice. 'But I would have preferred that he had just left, never to return.'

A heavy silence enveloped them.

Kate regarded her friends, seeing once again the toll Lincoln had taken on their lives, His departure was something she had never discussed with them. He had gone, and peace had entered her life. Had she been wrong in thinking they had also found peace?

What was Fletcher thinking? She had never seen him so … withdrawn and troubled.

When and if the body was identified as Lincoln's, she would carry on with her life, forever silently grateful to the person who had rid them all of the shadow that had hovered over their lives. She hoped that Fletcher and Nicole would be able to do the same.

'I'll go,' she said as she grasped her handbag and rose from the chair.

Nicole reached out a hand, anxiety clouding her eyes. 'Kate … the police … you won't …'

Fletcher sat forward, grabbed Nicole's other hand, stopping her. 'Never. You don't have to ask.'

Kate moved to Nicole's side, bent and placed a swift kiss on her cheek. 'Fletch is right … *never*,' she whispered. 'Stay well, both of you.' She then nodded to Fletcher and gratefully left the room.

There was too much emotion in that room, and Kate had enough of her own to deal with.

Just outside the room, a young man stood reading her friend's hospital chart, a look of concern and something else on his face, which Kate couldn't identify. *Horror*, she thought, then shook it away as being silly and fanciful. 'Anthony?' she queried.

He looked up, grey eyes, dark and unfocused, clouded with something Kate didn't recognise. 'Huh?'

'It is Anthony, isn't it?' Kate posed it as a question, but she would have known him anywhere; he looked so much like his father.

'Yes. Ah …' His eyes remained unfocused. 'Mrs Ayres? Oh yes, hi.' He slipped the hospital chart back into the box attached to the door. 'Ah, nice to see you again. I was just going into see Mum.' He sidestepped Kate and slipped in the room.

Kate wondered what it was about the chart that had bothered him so. She took the chart from its holder and flipped through it: temperature chart, medication chart, and there were others that Kate couldn't categorise, but she thought they were innocuous. None of the charts seemed to give out information that was concerning.

However, Anthony had seen something, and Kate could tell it disturbed him.

## Chapter Seven

# Fletcher

The moment his son stepped into the room, Fletcher knew something was bothering him. Anthony had never been able to hide his emotions, and Fletcher often wondered how he'd be able to deliver bad news to a patient when he became a doctor. Anthony's emotions had always been close to the surface, and that had helped Fletcher understand and parent him into the fine young man standing before them.

A glance at his wife's face told Fletcher that she was oblivious to their son's anxiety. He loved her, but over the years, he became increasingly aware of her ability to see only her pain and be totally unaware of the angst of those around her. Even now, she was in hospital, distraught over the finding of the body, and yet it was Kate and her boys who had been most affected by the cruelty of the man and the thought that he was killed in suspicious circumstances.

Fletcher knew that suspicion would surely land at everyone's doorstep.

Nicole hadn't even asked Kate how she was faring with all that was happening.

Fletcher pushed down his disappointment and focused on his son. 'Anthony? You okay?'

Anthony slumped into the nearest chair. Then suddenly, he stood again and walked to the corner of the hospital room. He backed into the corner and faced them. 'I've just read your chart, Mum. Your blood group is O positive and so's Dad's. Mine is B … so … am I adopted.'

'Oh shit,' Fletch whispered.

Nicole reached out and grabbed his hand and gasped. 'No! No! Fletch! Fletch!'

Holding onto Fletcher's hand, she reached out her other hand to her son. Tears cascaded down her face, and Fletcher had the ungracious thought that tears were sometimes a weapon too.

He pushed that thought aside and gently extricated himself from his wife's hand and rose to embrace his son, who was looking confused and hurt. 'Not adopted.' He sighed. 'I loved you from the moment you were born.' Fletcher felt Anthony's arms tighten around him and his head rest gently on his shoulder. As Anthony's breathing slowed and his body relaxed, Fletcher stepped back from his son and gazed into his eyes. 'You may not be my blood, but in my heart and soul, you're a part of me and always will be.' He watched as Anthony clearly processed what he had just told him.

Anthony nodded, but his eyes showed confusion. 'So, I'm Mum's but not yours?'

Fletcher grimaced and watched tears flood Anthony's eyes, then spill and flow down his face.

'I'm not *yours*. I'm not your *son*.' Anthony sobbed.

Fletcher caught Anthony as his knees buckled, and he held him until Anthony regained his feet. He then guided his son to a chair, where Anthony sat head in hand, his body shaking with the strengths of his sobs.

Nicole gazed with a look of helplessness at Fletcher and swung her feet over the side of the bed. 'But you're mine, Anthony. My son … I …love …'

Anthony lifted his head and stared at his mother. 'I don't want to be *just* yours,' he said fiercely. 'You've never loved me like Dad. You … you're … who? No, don't tell me, I don't want to know. I need to be alone … I want to think.' He stood, grabbed Fletcher into a fierce hug, then threw a disparaging glance at his mother before leaving the room.

Fletcher surveyed Nicole dispassionately as she dissolved into a fresh outburst of crying, knowing that her tears were only for herself and not for him or their son.

'How could he be so cruel? How could he say he didn't want to be *just* mine?' She sobbed.

'He's had a terrible shock, Nicole. I told you we needed to tell him earlier. I wish now I had never listened to you.'

'You should have let me tell him.' She wailed. 'You shouldn't have just jumped in and made it all about you.'

'Well … when you do talk to him, are you going to tell him the truth?'

'The truth? What do you mean by that?' Nicole's voice had risen to a level that was almost a screech.

Fletcher gazed at his wife with brooding eyes. He often wondered what the truth actually was.

The moment Nicole had told him she was pregnant, he knew the child she carried was not his.

They had been trying to have a child for the best part of three years, and before he broached the subject of infertility with her, he wanted to make sure he wasn't to blame so he had quietly consulted a doctor and found out that the problem lay with him. 'Poor motility … lower than average sperm count …' The words still reverberated inside his head and carried the power to stir the pain he carried deep inside. He had been trying to find the right words to tell Nicole that it was his fault they were failing to have a child.

Then she told him she was pregnant.

'I can't have children,' he had blurted. 'I've seen a doctor, and I've been trying to find a way to tell you.'

'No! No!' Nicole had screamed. 'It must be yours; it has to be. It can't be his. It can't be.'

At the sudden intrusion of the memory, Fletcher folded his arms and rubbed his face. *Christ!* He wished he was at home where it was easy to escape into doing something productive until the Nicole storm had passed, where he didn't have to continually cope with her emotional tsunamis. They had controlled her and shaped their lives ever since he told her he couldn't have children and that the child she carried was not his.

He now breathed in deeply through his nose and let the air out in a deep sigh.

'There you go! Huffing and puffing again. You always do that when you don't like what I say. You …'

Nicole's tirade was interrupted by the door abruptly opening and Anthony entering the room. 'Anthony … love …' Nicole began.

'Save it, Mum. I didn't go anywhere. As much as I wanted to run away, Dad taught me never to run from problems either physically or emotionally. I've been outside the door the whole time. Are you going to tell me the truth?'

'I … um … it's not that easy,' Nicole stammered.

'Not easy to "tell the truth", you mean?' questioned Anthony, his tone harsh.

Fletcher caught Ant's eye and shook his head in warning.

Anthony mirrored Fletcher by inhaling deeply and letting it rush out his nose.

Nicole gave a harsh snort of laughter. 'You may not carry his genes, but you certainly take after him.'

'He is my father in every way that counts, so of

course I take after him. I don't want to know why or how; I just want to know whose genes I do carry. I don't care if you had an affair, Mum. Dad has stayed with you all these years, so I figured he must have forgiven you.'

'It's not my fault. I can't … You can't just judge *me*,' Nicole snapped at him.

'Nothing's ever your fault, Mum. I've learnt that much. Just tell me his name. When I want to know more, I'll ask, but for now, I just want his name,' said Anthony through gritted teeth.

'Ant …' said Fletcher softly.

'What … be kind … isn't that what you always say when it comes to Mum?'

'Do you? Oh, Fletch. How lovely …'

'No, Mum. Stop! Just tell me his name, and then I'm going back to Sydney. I need to …'

'No, you can't just leave. Not like this. You can't be angry at *me*.'

'Then who should I be angry with? Dad? What for? Raising someone else's kid with love, like it was his own? What about me, Mum, what about what I need? Have you ever thought of that?'

Fletcher watched his wife and son's exchange, saw the need and desperation in Anthony and the utter lack of compassion in Nicole. He wanted to step in; he always stepped in, and maybe that was the problem, trying to save Nicole from herself.

But now, he felt the last vestige of protectiveness towards Nicole slip away and an overwhelming emptiness filled him, it was almost a relief to finally let go of the reins. What had he held onto all these years? He thought he had been protecting her out of love. But for whom? His wife or his son, who was now a man and could make his own decisions.

Fletcher saw the moment Anthony gave up trying to reach his mother and watched him turn to him.

'Do you know?' Anthony asked, his voice harsh with emotion. Tension had made his body rigid.

Fletch slowly nodded, and after several heartbeats, he replied, 'Lincoln Kelly.'

'What! What! Jane's father? *Jane's* father?' Ant looked as if he were going to vomit.

The silence that followed had an energy that swirled and charged around the room, touching each of its occupants.

A heavy stillness filled the room.

Fletcher watched his son's face grow pale and a dawning horror fill his eyes as he struggled to process what he had just learnt. Nicole reached out to Fletcher, but he kept his hands grasped firmly together and made no move to comfort her. He had no energy left to give her; his focus was entirely on his son, who he knew was silently putting pieces together in his mind.

'You sent me away because Jane and I were getting too close?' Anthony's eyes widened.

Fletcher felt his lower lip tremble. 'Yes.'

'You pretended you weren't friends with Jane's mum because what? You didn't want her mum to know?'

'She knows. She's known for a long time.' He held his son gaze, his eyes filled with regret.

'Does Jane know?'

'No … now stop! Stop this. You don't understand. He raped me,' Nicole exclaimed.

'For pity's sake, Nicole,' Fletcher exclaimed. 'He doesn't *have* to know that! Couldn't you just let him ask his questions? Just try for once to understand how someone else feels!'

'Of course, he needs to know!' retorted Nicole. 'He has to realise it wasn't *my* fault.'

Fletcher grimaced. Anthony was right, nothing was ever Nicole's fault. She was like a child and never took responsibility for anything.

'Raped you, Mum? Really?' interrupted Anthony.

Nicole gasped as if she had been struck and fell back against the pillows, her face white. Fletcher reached out to hold her, but with a swiftness he had seen too many times before, she launched herself from the bed and struck her son across the face.

Instinctively, Anthony leapt to his feet and pushed his mother away. She fell against the bed; unhurt, she quickly regained her balance. Her eyes blazed with a hatred from which both Anthony and Fletcher recoiled.

Fletcher was the first to act. 'Stop! Enough. Nicole, get back into bed,' he ordered.

Gently, he held his son's arm and led him from the room and out of the hospital and down to Anthony's car. 'I'm sorry, I wanted to tell you, but I didn't because your mum didn't want me to. You know how emotional she becomes if she doesn't get her own way. We'll talk later, son. Don't tell Jane or her brothers, not yet. I'll talk to Kate.'

'I'm not going home, Dad. I'll find a place to stay in town. I need time to think.'

Fletcher hugged his son goodbye and watched him drive away, and then he reluctantly turned his footsteps towards the hospital.

At the entrance, he paused; a few minutes later, he too was driving away with another memory forcing its way into his conscious mind …

Lincoln on his motorbike, riding fast, as always, and Fletcher on alert for the next time he rode through.

When the bike was close, too close for him to stop, Fletcher drove the tractor out in front of the motorbike.

Fletcher stood over Lincoln as he lay on the ground, arm broken, dazed and bleeding from several gashes. 'Touch my wife again and they'll never find your body.'

## Chapter Eight

# Jane

Mum was digging in the garden when I got home, a sure sign she needed to work off something that was bothering her. So, I decided I wouldn't add to that something by questioning her about what Shirley had told me. There would be another time for that. I then figured I must be maturing, because once I would have gone straight to her and demanded an answer. Now, as Uncle Arthur would say, I thought it best to 'let sleeping dogs lie'.

I decided I wouldn't talk to her of Ant or Shirley but maybe a safer topic like strange old Mrs Kelly, who didn't seem to care that her son may have been lying in a gully for the past twenty years. Had he been as mean to her as he seems to have been to other members of his family?

I replenished my supplies and packed the car ready for tomorrow, then I washed away the day's worries by having a long, hot shower.

Much later, after dinner was over and the brothers were watching television, Mum and I were sitting on the front deck, watching the sun splash colour across the evening sky before it dipped beneath the horizon. My phone buzzed with a message:

*Your services are no longer needed.*
*I shall employ another.*
*Regards, Mrs Kelly*

'Oh!' Disappointment raced through me.

'What?' Mum asked.

I read the text aloud and told her of my morning's encounter with the old woman. 'What do you know of her, Mum? Why haven't you had anything to do with her for all these years.'

'I didn't know you were working for her. You should have told me.'

'Mum! She was a client. You don't have to know all my clients.'

'Maybe so …' Mum started then stopped. 'Okay. Okay.' She sat in silence for so long I thought she wasn't going to answer me.

Inside, my brothers were yelling at the television, probably watching football, which I found totally unappealing, but I was becoming frustrated with her silence and was thinking of joining them … and then she spoke.

'Your father didn't want to invite her to our wedding, and he would never say why, so I sent her an invitation and she refused. He used to say, "she's no mother of mine", but I took that to mean he had disowned her or …' She paused. 'Vice versa. He also spoke very little about his childhood. His father left, I gathered when he was about ten years old. And then he died when Lincoln was about twenty, so he was gone long before I met your father.'

'She's very unhappy, Mum. I sort of feel sorry for her.'

Mum looked at me. 'You can't help her, sweetheart. I tried. After Sam was born, I took him to see her.

I knocked on the door, she opened it, and when she saw who it was, she shut the door in my face. I never went back. And when we see each other in the street, we both pretend we don't know one another. The boys know who she is and have never wanted to get it touch with her.'

'Why have you never told me any of this?' I exclaimed. 'Why have I been excluded so much? I thought it was because … well … because Dad left, and you were pregnant. I know it doesn't make sense, but there were times when I thought it was because of me.'

Mum grabbed me and pulled me from the chair into an embrace; she wasn't really a hugger, and it kind of shocked me.

For a moment, I stood in stunned silence before slowly wrapping my arms around her and relaxing into her arms. Tears stung my eyes, and she sniffed into my hair. 'Don't snot on me,' I said, and we pulled apart with a laugh.

She looked hard into my eyes and gave me a little shake. 'None of this is your fault. None of it, you hear. It's his and mine.'

We sat.

'Why yours?'

'Because I couldn't see what was under my nose ... or I didn't want to. I look back now and wonder how I could have been so blind. Why I didn't listen to my instincts.'

'Are you talking about ... what Max said? Why was Dad so mean?'

'I don't know, love. I've driven myself mad thinking about it, but I've decided it's a problem my mind can't solve. He was just mean. I do think there was a time when he tried to be different, but in the end, his anger or whatever it was just got the better of him, and he lashed out. Not so much at me, but the boys. He was very loving towards me, but apparently, that was one of the warning signs that he was about to turn mean ... the boys told me this long after he had gone. And I wasn't aware of it because he threatened them, he ... they told me later, much later ... he told them that if they said anything to me, he would kill me. So, they kept their silence. Outside the family, he seemed to be able to control his temper, not always but mostly ... then, occasionally, he slipped.'

'Shirley calls them "street angels and home devils".'

'You talked to Shirley?'

'A little,' I admitted, feeling slightly ashamed.

'It's okay, love.' Mum reached over and squeezed my hand.

Silence fell between us again, this time, soft and reassuring, and I thought: *silence has many faces.*

Eventually, I returned our conversation to Mrs Kelly.

'I was hoping she would talk to me and tell me why she didn't want to give the police her DNA,' I said.

'She will never tell you, and apart from not being in our circle of friends, I've never wanted to know. But if you do want to know more, I suggest you talk to Shirley a bit more. People confide in her because they know she doesn't spread gossip. She might know it all, but she doesn't spread it.'

'Does she know it all?'

'Believe me, there isn't much that Shirley doesn't know. Mind you, I doubt she knows anything about the body in the gully. That would be a miracle and put a lot of suspicion on Shirley.' Mum laughed.

I didn't, I was thinking about the small boy with the scars on his back. Mum had let me peek through a window into her earlier life, but I knew she wasn't ready to throw the door wide open and let me in. And for now, that was enough.

\*

Ant blew me off with a text the next day. I had been looking forward to seeing him again, but I didn't mind as much as I thought I would. Yesterday, I had been excited to see him, imagining all sorts of romantic trysts.

Overnight, my subconscious mind untangled everything, and I knew that whatever was between us, we would never work. He was very much the city man now, and I avoided cities like the plague. And the girl he talked about; I realised any sympathy that I felt the day before was gone.

Today, I wanted to slap him for being so … pathetic. His hormones (to be polite) were obviously leading him around by the nose, and I envisioned Ant's face on a bull with a ring in his snout.

I chuckled to myself and opened my insulated lunch bag that held my sandwiches, and then I poured a coffee from the thermos. I was glad to be alone.

Apart from a few other people taking their lunch break, the park was empty. During school holidays, it was not the place to be if one wanted to be alone with their thoughts, and I did want to be alone with my thoughts.

The trouble with thoughts, though, was that they tended to lead you up the garden path. I wanted to know my family's secrets, and yet I didn't want to know. I had been drifting along a path that I had never questioned, and now I was wondering if this was what I wanted to do with the rest of my life.

I liked cleaning homes; I liked helping people, but I wondered if there was something else I could or should be doing. Most of all, I liked being independent, and I didn't really want to work for someone else or work at someone else's pace. I had thought about expanding the business in the past and had always rejected the idea. Maybe it was time I revisited it seriously. It might also be time to consider my own place, not in town. I toyed with the idea of asking Mum to let me build my own place on the property.

I took a sip of a coffee and tried to think about how and where I could build. Despite that, my mind had other ideas … it wandered instead to an image of Max.

And once again, I saw the pain on his face the day the detectives came, it was enough to make me want to hide my head in the sand and never lift it out. But if I probed too deeply, would I find out that one of my family members was a killer?

Sam and Max were too young, they couldn't have done it.

Uncle Arthur didn't come to us until after Lincoln left, or so everyone said.

And as yet, I hadn't caught anyone in a lie, just secrets, so that left Mum, and even she would have needed help. I had been over the same dilemma in my mind previously and had come to the same conclusion.

*I have no idea.*

'Have you worked it out yet?' A familiar voice said from the other side of the table. Detective Sergeant Law slid into the seat opposite me.

'You're making a habit of that,' I told him. 'And worked out what?

Blue eyes held mine. 'Whatever it is that you're thinking about. You've been holding onto that sandwich and haven't taken a bite for quite a while now.'

'What do you want?'

A smile touched his eyes, but not his mouth, and I saw a kindness in him that I hadn't seen before. He was tough, but his strength lay in his gentleness.

'Sorry, I'm on a short fuse these days. I guess you're just doing your job ...' I grinned. 'So ... what *do* you want?' My tone was not so abrupt this time.

He chuckled. 'Are you always so blunt?'

'Pretty much. I was taught by two brothers who

don't take any prisoners. They usually tell it like it is.'

'Usually?' He was quick.

'Yeah, well, I'm learning … lots …' I studied him and then looked away.

He didn't pursue it, thankfully. 'If you want to learn more about Mrs Kelly, I suggest you look at the births, deaths and marriages registry.'

My interest sparked. 'Really?'

He nodded. 'I can't tell you anything more. It's not relevant to our investigation, but it does explain some of her reluctance to speak to us and provide her DNA.'

'She sacked me last night, by text. I didn't realise she was so tech-savvy; though her mind seems to be stuck in the past.'

'Yeah … well, people like to run away from things instead of facing them,' said the sergeant.

'Maybe some things are difficult to face,' I told him.

He was easy to talk to, and I had to stop myself from discussing my thoughts further.

His eyes narrowed, and he said almost reluctantly, 'A forensic anthropologist is looking at the skeleton. Hopefully, that should tell us "cause of death". And I don't know how long the DNA will take. Apparently, it's dependent on several different things that only a scientist could explain. When we know more, I'll let the rest of your family know. In the meantime, you can pass on what I've just told you. Or not,' he said before he got up from his seat and walked away.

That evening, Mum dug through some of her old papers and eventually came up with Lincoln's birth certificate. It showed his mother as being 'Hazel Jones', and his father 'Unknown'. However, I knew Mrs Kelly as Margaret, not Hazel.

Over the next couple of weeks, I spent hours and money researching the various government and genealogy websites and discovered that Lincoln had been adopted by Margaret and Parker Kelly. His birth mother was Margaret's younger sister, Hazel.

Margaret and Parker divorced in 1966 when Lincoln was five years old, but that same year, Parker married Hazel.

With this knowledge, I visited Shirley.

'What made you start looking into Margaret's life?' she queried.

'Detective Law, he suggested it. Mrs Kelly refused to have her DNA checked against the body found in the gully, and she didn't want me to call her anything except Mrs Kelly.'

'Ah. So, he set you on a path to find your own answers.'

I nodded and took another bite of the delicious pumpkin cake Shirley had made.

'Do you know if Hazel is still alive, and if so, where I can find her?'

Shirley sipped her tea and sat staring into space; I knew she was deciding what and if she would tell me.

Eventually, she divulged, 'I can tell you that she is still alive, and the best way to find her address is through the electoral role. However, I'm not convinced that the woman would want to see you.'

'Shir … ley.' I groaned. 'She's my grandmother.'

'Yes, and one who never wanted to be in your life, or to know anything about you,' she said bluntly.

That shut me down. So, I took a deep breath and tried another tack. 'Did you *know* she was my grandmother?'

'Not until now. You have unveiled a long-held secret, and one that was the subject of some very nasty gossip back in the day. Now, it appears it wasn't just gossip, it held more than a kernel of truth.' She paused and drank her tea; it wasn't until she was looking at the bottom of an empty cup and returned it to the saucer before she continued. 'What I will tell you is this. Margaret and Hazel went to …' Shirley made air quotes with her fingers. '"Take care of an elderly aunt", and when they came home, Margaret had a baby in her arms. Of course, the gossips put two and two together, but nothing could be proven. Then a few short years later, she and Parker divorced, leaving her to bring up the child on her own. To make matters worse, Parker married Hazel, and as the child grew older, he began to look very much like Parker. It amazes me now that Parker and Hazel didn't take the child as well, seeing as he was their own.' Shirley poured herself another cup of tea and sat sipping for a while.

I wanted her to hurry up but decided it best if I held my tongue. She was likely to clam up if I tried to push her.

A long sigh escaped her lips, one that held more than a touch of frustration. 'If you do find her, think very carefully before you blunder in and go and see her,' Shirley warned.

She knew me too well. Of course, I wanted to see her.

'She is your grandmother in blood only,' Shirley continued in a more severe tone. 'She has not earnt that title. And I shudder at the selfishness of someone who has a baby to her sister's husband, then abandons the child and the sister in favour of the husband.'

'Yes, but.'

'No! No buts. You can't go trampling over people's lives just because you think you have the right to know.'

Hurt must have showed on my face, because Shirley's face and tone softened, and her body relaxed. 'Jane, this is someone's pain we're talking about. It's your family, and I know you want to know, and you think you have the right to know, but you don't. Consider Margaret Kelly … she has become a bitter old woman. Her pain has twisted her. And her sister never once acknowledged her son as her own. Not once. I would advise you to let it go.'

I sat back in my chair and stared at the wall. 'I wonder if Lincoln knew.' I murmured, more to myself than Shirley, but she answered.

'A child raised under those circumstances would have to be dearly loved to escape irreparable harm.'

I smiled at her. 'Thank you, Shirley. I'm curious … but I'll think long and hard about going to see Hazel. That's supposing, of course, that I can find her.'

'That's all I can ask, my dear. Sometimes, the most powerful thing we can do is to be silent.'

## Chapter Nine

# Kate

Autumn arrived, though summer still exerted a strong influence on the weather. The morning was hot, and it felt to Kate as if it was going to be hotter. She was hanging washing on the line when she saw a familiar car pull into the driveway and make its way to the house.

Expecting Fletcher, she was surprised when a young man alighted from the car. Her breath left her with a gasp as a frisson of fear knifed through her. An instant later, her body relaxed; apart from the brown hair, Anthony's features had her ex-husband stamped all over them. Thankfully, he walked like Fletcher, and that helped to dispel the illusion that it was Lincoln who walked towards her.

She watched as he approached. There was reluctance and a cautiousness in each step. He nodded and gave her a tight grin.

'Anthony? This is a surprise. What brings you all the way out here?' Kate said with a smile. She could feel the nervous energy coming off him in waves. 'Is your mum, okay? I haven't seen her since she came out of hospital.'

'Hi, Mrs Kelly.' Anthony shook his head. 'Sorry, it's not, is it? It's Ayres. Sorry. Uh, no Mum's fine … I just wanted to talk to you about … something …' His voice trailed off uncertainly.

'Alright, we can talk while I finish hanging this washing on the line.' Kate turned to retrieve another item from the basket and said, 'How can I help you?'

'Has Dad been in touch with you?'

Kate looked back at him. 'No. Why?'

'Ah, he said he would.'

Kate heard worry and a cautiousness in his tone and said, 'Look, let me finish this. Go to the verandah and take a seat. I'll be with you shortly, and we'll be able to talk properly.'

As Anthony disappeared around the corner of the

house, Kate took her phone from her pocket and texted Fletcher:

*Anthony here*
*What's going on?*

A brief reply came back:

*He knows.*
*Be honest with him.*
*Talk later.*

*Shit! Shit! Shit! Be honest?* Kate's thoughts screamed.

There were things she had never told Fletch, so how could she be honest with Anthony?

Kate slowly hung the rest of the washing on the line, her mind racing.

What in the world *was* she going to tell him?

Certainly not the truth, no one needs to hear that about their mother.

'Would you like something cold to drink?' she asked Anthony once they were inside. 'I'm not a wine drinker, but Jane is, so I have some white wine in the fridge, and I think there's some beer.'

'Cold water is fine, thanks Mrs Ayres. I'm driving.'

'Call me Kate. I'm not old, but calling me Mrs Ayres makes me feel old, and its Ms, anyway.' Kate smiled at him in what she hoped was a reassuring manner. Inside, she was trying to hold her nerves together and hoped it didn't show on her face. She was glad to see her hands were steady as she poured two glasses of water. Her hands were her giveaway when she was nervous. 'So, tell me what brings you out here and why; you seem a bit anxious.'

'Do I?' Anthony made a *humph* noise in his throat. 'Yeah, well ... I am a bit. I've recently found out that ... well Dad's told me that ... I've just found out that Dad's not my biological father.' He paused, swallowed, took a deep breath and plunged on. 'That I'm not his son,' he finished with a rush and a catch in his voice.

Kate could tell he was struggling to hold back the tears.

'And ... Mum said ... she was ... raped,' he said the words slowly, spacing each of them with a long pause between.

Kate breathed deeply; the face before her and the word 'rape' ignited an old recording ...

'Rape. That's a bit harsh, though she did need some persuading in the beginning,' Lincoln's voice sneered. 'After that she loved it, couldn't get enough, and the rougher the better. And you know what? After the vanilla sex that we have, so did I. She liked to be hurt, and I loved hurting her. What about you, Kate? Do you secretly like to be hurt?'

Kate feigned a cough and reached blindly for the glass of water in front of her. The first gulp sent her into a coughing fit. When she recovered, Kate placed the glass gently on the table and sat for a moment gathering her thoughts. 'What exactly do you want to know, Anthony. I'm not sure I'm the right person to be having this conversation with. Have you talked to your parents?'

'I've tried but … Mum has a meltdown every time I try to talk to her. And Dad … I don't know … but there seems to be something that he …' Anthony faltered, clearly struggling for the words to explain what it was that he wanted to know.

Watching him, Kate realised he just wanted to talk to someone who would listen to how he felt, and she knew that Fletcher and Nicole's own emotions were too deep and entangled to help their son wade through the confusion and hurt of suddenly finding out the truth about his parentage. 'When did you find out and how?' asked Kate.

Anthony explained to her about reading his mother's chart at the hospital.

'Couples who have Group O positive can only have children that are Group O, like themselves. And I'm B positive.'

'I see,' murmured Kate. 'So was Lincoln.'

'What was he like?'

Kate squirmed in her seat and gazed compassionately at the young man in front of her. 'Don't,' she whispered. 'Don't think about your biology. Think about the man who raised you. Fletcher is a fine man, and he would never have done what Lincoln did.'

'So, you really think … are you sure Mum didn't have an affair with your husband. There's something she's not saying, I know there is. No, that's not it.' Anthony shook his head. 'Well … yes, it is … sort of,' he finished lamely. 'Can you just tell me what you know,' he pleaded.

Kate took a deep breath and sifted through her memory, trying to work out exactly what she could tell him. She could still hear, even after all this time, Nicole's sobbing …

*

'I'm so ashamed, how could I have allowed it to happen? I told him no, but he wouldn't listen. Then he kept coming back, and I didn't know what to do.'

Kate had gazed at Nicole, wondering why she had chosen after all this time to tell the truth; she had no idea what to say.

So, she said nothing, and after a moment of silence, Nicole continued, 'He hit me. It wasn't hard, but he told me I had to be a good girl … and I just gave in. It reminded me so much of my father when he used to hit my sisters and I and tell us we had to be good girls.'

'Why are you telling me this? Lincoln has been gone for several months now,' interrupted Kate. A knot had formed in her stomach, and she felt sick at hearing of Lincoln's brutality, but she was also annoyed that Nicole used her to release her own emotions when she must have known that Kate herself struggled with her own demons where Lincoln was concerned.

'I need to talk to someone, but I don't want to talk to a stranger about something so personal. I don't think they would understand.'

'I think they are trained to understand and help,' Kate suggested softly and watched with concern as Nicole silently shook her head …

*

The soft thump of a glass as it touched the table brought Kate back to Anthony. Again, she was racking her brain trying to think what to say, and then she realised she didn't have to say anything, she just had to listen to a young man's pain. 'There are only two people who know exactly what happened, and one of them is dead, and you can't dig around in a very old wound without causing a great deal of harm. So … I can't tell you anything about that … Can you tell me what hurts you the most?' Kate asked him.

'Being lied to all these years … Dad said he wanted to tell me, but Mum didn't, and as usual, Dad gave into her. She's so manipulative. She throws a tantrum if she doesn't get her own way.'

'Does she, um … er, I wasn't aware of that,' Kate murmured, though his words triggered something deep in her subconscious. Had she been used by Nicole?

'Well, you wouldn't, would you? Dad protects her, and he's pretty good at hiding things, but I think even he is getting tired of it.'

Kate gazed at Anthony, not sure how to continue, but wishing she could find the words. It had crossed her mind once or twice that Nicole's behaviour was manipulative, but she had dismissed the idea and berated herself for being so judgemental and not being understanding enough.

Now Kate was wondering if by divulging some of what had passed between Lincoln and herself, Nicole hadn't ensured that Kate herself bore some of the guilt and responsibility. *That's crazy, and I'm not sure how that works,* she contemplated, but she felt an acknowledgment of truth ignite within her as another memory moved through her mind …

'I don't think you understand. I feel guilty and ashamed because I … I started to enjoy his … his visits,' Nicole had said softly.

'He told me,' replied Kate, unable to keep an edge out of her voice. 'In fact, he bragged about it, but I didn't think it was true because you had told Fletcher and I that it had only happened once, and we believed you.'

'He … told … you? What must you think of me? Please don't tell Fletcher.'

'You know I wouldn't hurt Fletch. And as for what I think of you? Apart from you both being married, Lincoln's cruelty and disrespect for all of us is appalling. I feel numb at the moment, so I don't think anything of you, specifically, and I can't pretend to understand or condone what took place between the two of you. In other circumstances, I believe that everyone is different, and if what happens is between consenting adults, then it's none of my business. The problem is, I'm not sure how much was consensual between the two of you and how much you believe it was …

Now, Kate was wondering if perhaps there had been more consent than what she assumed.

Anthony became silent, and Kate could see his internal struggle with something … She guessed and asked, 'Are you wondering about Jane and your brothers?'

Tears flooded Anthony's eyes, and Kate's eyes responded with tears also.

'Do you want them to know?' he asked.

'Of course. I would have told them years ago, when you and Jane had first taken such a liking to each other, but it wasn't my choice. I had to respect your mother's wishes. She was so upset, and I didn't want to …' Kate faltered – was not that a perfect example of how Nicole had influenced both her and Fletcher? Neither had thought of how Martha or Anthony felt. They had been separated without explanation or concern for anyone but Nicole.

'I'm sorry. We should have told you both. I see now that it was a mistake.'

'*She* would never have told me. And Dad *always* gives in to her.' Anthony said staring down at the table. There was a bitterness in his voice that tugged at Kate's heart.

'She's so self-protective, she doesn't see anyone else. Not Dad, not me. Jane and I ... we could have ... it could have hurt us both so badly.' Anthony stopped looking up at Kate, as if realising he had said too much. 'I ... I could have had brothers and ... a ... sister—' He broke off with a sob, clearly struggled to regain control, sniffed and continued, 'Can I tell Jane?'

'Yes. And I'll tell Sam and Max. We'll see how everyone feels, and then we'll go from there. At some time, maybe you can all get together here. Would you like that?'

Anthony nodded his head, a gleam of hope in his eyes. 'Thank you so much. I can't tell you how much this means to me.'

*You're wrong*, thought Kate. *I can see how much it means, and stuff Nicole for allowing Lincoln to win and keeping everyone apart all these years.*

## Chapter Ten

# Jane

I hadn't heard from Ant for a couple of weeks, though thoughts of him popped into my head every now and then as I worked. My phone calls went unanswered, and so did my text messages. Busy with work and having decided to look for help with the business, the days slipped by almost unnoticed.

Also, subtle changes were taking place within the family, which I felt more than saw anything concrete. Mum had been quiet all evening and wasn't at breakfast; my brothers said she had gone for a long, early morning walk. They, for some unknown reason, were hanging around the house having a leisurely breakfast (this in itself was very strange). I looked at each in turn, and they might as well have been cast in stone, for all their faces gave away.

It didn't add up to much, but there was definitely something in the air.

The weather hadn't changed. Summer maintained its grip on the climate while autumn attempted to assert itself with a cool breeze, but even that proved futile.

Despite the weather, I wanted to find a shady tree and eat my lunch in the park, but I had put ads online and in the local paper for a part-time employee. I had also asked my clients to recommend someone, and today I sat in the local café waiting to interview two candidates for the position.

The decision to expand had taken me a long time to make, and I felt a sense of excitement that I had finally taken the step.

I ordered a coffee and waited … and waited – the first candidate didn't show. So, I ordered lunch and had just finished when someone plonked themselves into the chair opposite me.

'Mar … ta,' she crooned.

*Oh, crap.* I thought I had recognised the name. Lisa

Andrews sat before me. Blonde, blue eyes, beautiful with long painted talons. I hadn't liked her in school, and she had done nothing so far to change that.

'It's Mar … *tha*.' I said coolly. 'And you know very well that I prefer Jane.'

'Hmm, yes,' she murmured. '*P … l … ain* Jane, that's right.'

'Are you really applying for this position, Lisa?' I said bluntly.

'Well, yes … you see, that's part of the Centrelink agreement. I *have* to apply for jobs, however mundane.'

I wanted to throw my coffee in her face but amused myself by envisioning her with coffee dripping off that beautiful hair and running down her face, ruining her carefully applied make-up. 'Well, you've had an interview, so now be on your way,' I told her.

'Okay. Toodle-loo!' She rose, waved her talons at me and sauntered off.

*Toodle-loo! Toodle-loo! Who in their right mind says that! Where did she get that word from? Her great-grandmother?*

People like Lisa exhausted me; they only ever saw themselves. What a waste of a morning. I had rearranged my appointments for nothing. I might as well have stayed at home and put my feet up and had a glass of wine.

Instead, I ordered another coffee and thought about what I was going to do next. Obviously, finding the right person was not going to be so easy. I stared off into space and sipped my coffee.

A woman, who had been sitting in the café for as long as I had, approached me.

'Um, sorry, I couldn't help overhearing you, but are you looking to hire someone. Can I ask you what for?'

The woman before me was about thirtyish, with mousy-brown hair. She was short and round with the most beautiful clear skin. Stress showed clearly around her eyes and in the timid way in which she stood before me, grasping the back of the chair as if for support.

'Sure,' I said. 'Sit down.' I indicated the chair she was holding onto as if her life depended on it. 'I run my own cleaning business, and I was hoping to expand, but it's going to be harder than I thought.'

'Would you consider me?'

'Why not,' I replied.

*

An hour later, we parted, and I had my very first employee. Laura had a spring in her step and a smile on her face. Tomorrow, being Saturday, she was going to come to the house so I could give her some equipment for when she was ready to kick off on her own. Come Monday, we would work together until I thought she was ready to work alone, and then I would give her a list of clients.

I was standing at my car when a familiar voice spoke close to me.

'Jane?'

Standing a few feet back from me was Ant.

'Ant,' I squealed. 'What the hell has happened to you?'

Gone was the citified young man I had seen only a couple of weeks ago. Ant was dressed in an old T-shirt that looked like it should be in the ragbag, or better still the bin, and had on faded blue jeans and rubber thongs. Not classy leather thongs but *rubber* thongs. *Very un-Ant like*, I thought. His hair looked like it needed a good wash as well as a comb.

'What's happened?' I moved to grab his hand, but he pulled away.

'We … I … can we talk?' he stammered.

This made me all the more worried.

Not giving him an opportunity to avoid me, I grasped his arm firmly and moved him away from the car and across the road towards the park.

We walked for a while, with me taking quick surreptitious glances at him.

He had definitely been crying. His body was rigid with stress, and he smelt … off. *Had he not bathed?* I wrinkled my nose.

I guided him towards a huge ancient camphor laurel tree. It was wide and shady, and I had always thought that a sense of peace emanated from it.

We stopped in front of it, and I pushed him towards the tree.

'Uncle Arthur is weird sometimes, but he is never wrong. Go hug the tree or stand beside it, or do whatever you like, but don't come and talk to me until you've gained some of the tree's stillness.' I left him then and walked over to a park bench and sat, trying to still my own worries and be ready to listen to Ant.

I waited and watched and saw the changes move through Ant's body. Finally, he stepped back, found me with his eyes and made his way over to where I sat.

Thankful that we were sitting side by side and not facing each other, I listened in horror as he told me that the man who had fathered me was not only a rapist but had also fathered him.

My mouth closed with a snap, and it was then I became aware that it had been open. 'Shit,' I whispered. 'Shit.' I reached for his hand, and he allowed me to take it.

A long silence fell between us as he let me process what he had just told me.

'Oh God! Oh my God, that means my brother was the first boy to feel my tits!' I squeaked. I turned to face him then. 'Anthony, we almost ... we almost ...' I couldn't finish, but he knew what I meant.

'I know. Mum was so busy protecting herself, her silence could have bloody well destroyed us,' Ant said, pain and disgust in his voice.

'Why didn't your dad and my mum say anything?'

'Protecting Mum. Dad's always protecting Mum, and so was your mum. Too bloody bad about us.' The bitterness was strong in his voice.

'Remember we talked about running away together when they were going to send you to boarding school?' I asked.

'Worse,' he said. 'Do you remember what else we thought we would do?'

'Yes,' I whispered. 'Get me pregnant. It was only the thought of my brothers that stopped us.'

'Thank Christ for that,' he said vehemently.

We looked at each other and laughed.

He then asked hesitantly, 'Do you mind?'

'Mind what?'

'That I'm your half-brother?'

'Why should I mind? Now I understand why we've always felt such a strong connection. We just misinterpreted what the connection was. And you are my brother, forget about the half.'

'What do you think Sam and Max are going to say?' he asked.

'Well, as long as we don't tell them you groped me, they'll be fine.' I laughed and punched him lightly in the arm.

We strolled back to my car, arm in arm, happy, and I realised that Sam and Max were more authoritative father-figures in my life, but Ant was a friend and confidante. The kind of brother I always wanted.

## Chapter Eleven

# Kate

Kate hadn't meant to walk this way. When she set out, her intention had been to go for a long morning walk to clear her head, to try to find the words to explain to her sons that they had a brother and that she had known about him before Jane was born. She tried hard not to keep secrets from them. However, between them, they had kept too many secrets from Jane, and she often thought that the agreement they had made to shield her had been a mistake. She knew too well how other people's secrets and their insistence on silence frequently impacted negatively on the lives of others.

Her feet, on the other hand, had had other ideas and they, seemingly on their own volition, choose the bush track that led to Arthur's place.

In days gone by, Kate knew that Arthur would have been seen as a mystic and a healer. Today, he was some weird old man who lived a hermit's life in the bush.

In her heart, she was glad she was following the path to Arthur's place; there were things that needed to be said, so that she could hear them out loud and maybe make some sense of them.

The birds fell silent at her approach and began their song again after she passed. Arthur would know he was to receive an early morning visitor, and Kate hoped he would have put the kettle on; she had forgone her early morning coffee in favour of an immediate start to her walk.

Better still, she hoped he had lit a campfire and put the billy on – tea with a hint of wood smoke was the best.

She had told the boys to wait at home for her, she needed to talk to them, and she knew they would. They were more in tune to her moods than Jane. Jane, thankfully, had been untouched by her father's shadow, yet she was resilient and old enough now not to be affected too deeply by what she may learn.

She pondered briefly on how Anthony's talk with Jane would go. Kate was sure that for a moment, Jane would be horrified, and then her sense of humour would take over. The problem would come if Jane continued to hold romantic feelings for Anthony. She hoped not, just as she hoped she hadn't been wrong in the belief that their first love infatuation had not led to a more intimate connection.

Arthur was sitting on a log beside the campfire when Kate entered the clearing. As she approached, he reached into a can, took out a handful of tea leaves and threw them into the billy before taking it off the fire to steep.

He nodded at her, and she gave him a small smile in greeting. The dogs gave her an enthusiastic welcome before finally settling and returning to their usual resting places, where they lay, head on paws and watched.

'I've made bread. No butter, but you can have syrup, jam or honey. There's bacon, if you want.'

'Bacon, please,' said Kate. 'And then syrup.' Hunger had caught up with her.

She watched as Arthur set about making breakfast; his movements were slow, deliberate, and Kate thought there was something calming about the way he moved and conducted himself.

Finally, he placed in her hand a plate with a thick slice of homemade bread and two pieces of bacon with lots of fat. A mug of tea, which she usually took black, to which a tablespoon of condensed milk had been added, was placed beside her.

'You need it,' he said, and any objection she may have made died before leaving her lips.

When she was sated, relaxed, and a feeling of deep peace occupied every cell in her body, he said, 'Tell me ...'

The boys were red with sunburn, hatless and dehydrated when he bought them home. She had been standing on the verandah, watching the ute make its way towards the house. There was something off in its approach, too slow, she thought. He didn't usually drive so slowly. How many times had she told him to be more mindful of the boys as they bounced around in the cabin of the vehicle, too small to brace themselves, and there was only one seatbelt.

She waited, shading her eyes against the glare. The sun was low on the horizon, but its rays were harsh still; the day had been a scorcher. Kate had been surprised that they had stayed out in it all day. Fencing was hard work, and Sam and Max were too young to be of much help. They were with him for company only and the occasional fetch and carry.

A knot started somewhere in the pit of her stomach. Lately, that knot was a familiar visitor, and it was telling her something was wrong and had been for a long time.

Trouble was, she couldn't quite see what the problem was.

Lincoln, to her, was loving, attentive, though occasionally his words were cruel, but he was always apologetic, and she forgave him each time.

Lately, however, she had caught glimpses of fear in the way the animals approached him, and the other day, she thought he had tossed Sam off the verandah. They had both denied it, but something in Max's face told her they were lying.

Now, Lincoln was taking the car to the shed, something he wouldn't normally do. Her feet flew down the stairs, and she ran, her heart pounding inside her chest as a sense of dread gripped her.

When the ute came to a stop, she was beside it and ripped the door open to find Max curled up in a ball in the well of the passenger side and Sam struggling to both undo the seatbelt and release himself from his father's grip.

'What have you done,' she demanded of Lincoln. Anger was slow to come to Kate, but when it came, it was cold, implacable and deep.

Lincoln's face was a study in a swift range of emotions: shock, fear, indignation, and then it finally settled on a fight between contrition and defensiveness. It was as if he was searching for the right emotion to display.

Kate helped Sam to escape the seatbelt and his father's proximity, then she scooped Max up in her arms.

Inside, Kate ran a cool bath and, despite their feeble protests, undressed the boys and settled them into the bath.

Lincoln hovered. 'Kate, I didn't know they weren't drinking water? You have to believe me.'

'This took time, it didn't *just* happen,' she snarled as she pushed past him. She then headed to the kitchen and gathered up aloe vera for their sunburn and mixed electrolytes into a large jug of water, which she placed in the fridge.

On her return, she found Lincoln kneeling beside the bathtub, whispering heatedly to the boys.

'Get out!' Kate pulled hard on Lincoln's shirt, and he fell backwards.

'Mum! No. Don't … he'll … he'll hurt you too,' Sam croaked, fear in his eyes.

'Get out!' she screamed at Lincoln.

Lincoln scrambled to his feet, and Kate pushed him out the door before slamming it …

Kate stretched, cramped from sitting on the log. The mug in her hand had grown cold, and she threw the remaining tea into the bush.

'Go for a walk and settle. I'll make us another cup of tea,' Arthur told her.

While he fed the fire and set about making another billy of tea, Kate wandered through the bush, inhaling the scents of the forest and listening to the cicadas drone their relentless song. The birds had obviously decided that being with Arthur, she was no longer a threat. Their songs echoed throughout the bush, filling it with the sounds of their music.

Another slice of bread with syrup this time and a fresh cup of tea later, Kate was ready to continue.

'The boys recovered slowly, and I kept them close.

They didn't go out with Lincoln again. I … I eventually told Lincoln that he had to leave.' Kate took a deep breath and met Arthur's eyes. 'He … he had a complete meltdown. He started yelling that he couldn't leave. That this was his home. He pleaded and cried. God, he was screaming, really. It was one of the scariest things I'd ever seen.'

Arthur nodded his understanding, and Kate saw compassion in his eyes. And even though he turned his gaze back to the fire, Kate knew that his entire being was focused on her.

She breathed several deep, calming breaths before continuing, 'About a month or so later, I took them to visit Fletcher and Nicole. I really wanted to talk to Fletch about Lincoln. I had to get him off the station, but I was also worried about his mental health. My plan had been to leave the boys with them while I went and talked to a solicitor about how to go about things.' Kate shifted restlessly on the log. 'Their little boy was about three by then, and I hadn't seen him for quite a while. At the time, I didn't realise they were stopping me from seeing the child. I had seen him when he was a baby, but very little of him since then. Fletch would flag me down on my way into town, and we would have a chat, but we were both busy, and I never went inside their house or saw Nicole or Anthony.'

Arthur whistled to the dogs and they immediately left their resting spots and came toward him with tongues lolling and tails wagging. Once close to Arthur, they sat and he gave each of them a piece of bacon. After devouring the bacon, the dogs waited, eyes bright with the anticipation of a second piece. Arthur shook his head and they turned unhurriedly and made their way back to their resting places.

Kate sipped at the hot tea and stared into the fire. Silence settled around them like a warm blanket until Kate spoke again. 'We were sitting outside in the shade, enjoying a cool drink and chat. The boys were all playing together, and that's when I realised how much they all looked alike, and that Anthony was Lincoln's child …'

Driving home from Fletcher and Nicole's had been a nightmare. A melange of emotions knifed through Kate as she negotiated the bush roads. Random events rose unbidden in her mind, incidents that she had not connected before.

He had been loving and persuasive, at first.

And then there was their first fight.

'Add my name, honey, please. I've worked hard, and I'll work harder knowing that I have a financial interest in this place.'

'My family has worked this property for generations, Lincoln. Three years of hard work doesn't give you the right to a financial interest.'

'So, I'm to work for nothing, is that it?'

'If you call clothing you, feeding you, giving you money in the bank, a new car, motorbike … nothing,' Kate had retorted.

Anger sent his normally blue eyes black. Kate didn't think he knew it, but when he was angry, a dark film shuttered his eyes. 'So, what's it really about? Control. Is that it? I'm to be the lapdog, panting for handouts, is that it?'

'No. But Dad was right, he said after he died, the first thing you would do would be to ask for your name to be put on the deeds.' Suddenly angry at his senseless accusations, Kate chided, 'And he asked me to promise that I wouldn't.'

The moment the words were out of her mouth, Kate knew she had made a mistake.

Lincoln had recoiled as if struck. The darkness left his eyes, but something else replaced it, something she couldn't identify.

The following morning, Lincoln had returned to his normally loving self.

'Sorry, love.' He embraced her. 'You're right, I'm more than compensated for my work. I have you and the little tiger that's growing in your belly, what more could I want.' He had crooned in her ear.

But Blue, her ginger cat and who had been in Kate's life for fifteen years, was missing.

Similar incidents and other animals she loved suddenly went missing or were so badly hurt that she had to make the decision to have them put down.

All the fights and injured, lost or sick animals passed through her mind, and she knew with a dawning horror that that was what her body had been trying to tell her for so long.

'Don't come into the house just yet. Your father and I have something to discuss,' she told the boys when they arrived home.

On the ground, the shadows were lengthening. The sun was slowly making its way towards the horizon.

Lincoln was sitting at the kitchen table when Kate

entered the house. The remnants of a meal were in front of him. Unwashed dishes filled the sink, it was as if he had used every pot and pan in the house.

'How's lover boy.' He sneered.

*His veneer has well and truly slipped*, thought Kate as she stood watching him. Loathing rose inside of her. 'Pack your bags and leave,' she told him bluntly. 'I know what you did to Nicole.'

'And just what did I do to Nicole that she didn't want me to do?' He laughed. All pretence gone.

'You raped her, Lincoln, and I want you out of here. Now!'

'Raped her! That's rich. Maybe … just maybe I had to … shall we say "persuade" her … at first. But after that, she loved it.' He was on his feet and facing her, legs wide apart, aggression radiating from him like a black cloud; it surrounded him, making him look even more threatening.

*After that*, the words echoed in Kate's mind. 'It wasn't just once?' Kate asked, feeling weak; her legs had started to shake.

Lincoln's laugh was cruel, mocking. 'Is that what she said, that it happened only once?' he jeered.

A sick feeling began in her gut and slowly permeated

Kate's whole body. Nicole had said once, hadn't she, or had she just led Fletcher and Kate to believe it had been the one time. Kate was no longer sure, her mind raced trying to remember what Nicole had said. Maybe it was what she *hadn't* said? 'You're lying,' Kate said roughly. 'And if you're not, you're a pig.'

'I'm not lying,' he said softly, mockingly. He then took a step towards her, and Kate grabbed a knife from the table.

'Stay away,' she warned him.

'You're not going to do too much damage with that,' he said as he lunged towards her.

Kate grabbed a chair and hauled it between them, blocking his leap. He became tangled in the chair and fell to the floor. Kate picked up another chair and hit him hard.

Touching her pocket to make sure the keys to the car were still there, Kate turned and fled from the house.

She was running towards the car, yelling at the boys to come when something hard hit her from behind and everything went black …

\*

'That's what you've never told them,' said Arthur, bringing Kate back to the present. 'You never told them what triggered him off.'

Kate slowly shook her head. 'No. I just told them he had done something really bad to someone else and that I had confronted him.'

'And when you woke?' prompted Arthur.

'When I woke, I couldn't find the boys at first. Mind you, I was pretty groggy. Sam and Max told me later that he had punched me a few times while I was unconscious. Anyway, I eventually found Sam. He tried to run away and got caught up in the barbwire fence, and Lincoln whipped him with a stockwhip.' Kate took a deep breath, tears welled up in her eyes and she brushed them away. She had cried too much in the past. She was done with crying. 'Max got away,' she said softly.

## Chapter Twelve

# Jane

The mood in the house when I arrived home that evening … was odd. Not strained exactly, but there was a tense silence that was not normally there. Also, Mum hadn't started dinner, and Uncle Arthur was there.

'Uncle Arthur!' I said in surprise.

'Martha.' He nodded at me.

As I walked past, I rolled my eyes. *Again with the 'Martha', you annoying old git*, I thought.

'Bad thoughts lead to bad deeds, child,' said Uncle Arthur.

I backtracked and faced him. 'You're really scary, you know that?' I told him.

He smiled his little enigmatic smile, and I rolled my eyes again – this time he saw me, and his smile widened.

My gaze found my brothers. Max was staring at the television, supposedly watching a programme that I knew he hated. Sam was sitting beside him, engrossed in his mobile, his thumbs working furiously.

It was a bit difficult to tell everyone that I had a new employee and a new brother when sombre seemed to be the tone of the hour. But I thought, *bugger it*. 'I've employed someone,' I proclaimed.

'Good for you, Janey,' said Sam, not taking his eyes off his phone.

'Her name is Laura, and she has a five-year-old son,' I told the room, because no one else was listening. 'She's coming out on Saturday to pick up some gear, so I want you all to be on your best behaviour.'

That should have got a response, but it didn't.

So, I asked, 'Where's Mum?'

Silence.

'Where … is … Mum?' Louder this time.

'Garden,' Max mumbled.

'Oh! O … kay then,' I muttered and wandered off

to my room to shower. If Mum was in the garden this late in the afternoon and not in the kitchen, she was stressed or … something. Had the talk with Sam and Max about Ant gone wrong?

Feeling fresher after a shower, I returned to the living room.

Still no Mum.

'Anyone hungry?'

'Not really,' someone mumbled.

'Okay then … how does pasta with creamy mushroom sauce sound?'

Crickets.

'Well, that's what you're getting.'

I wasn't in the kitchen long before Mum joined me.

'I've put the apple pie that was in the fridge, in the oven, if you'd like to make some custard,' I told her.

We worked in silence.

Mum was calm – whatever had upset her had obviously passed. After she made the custard, she set the table and called the men.

I served them up crunchy salad and then some pasta with creamy mushroom sauce. They seemed to have forgotten they weren't hungry.

As we ate, the mood that I had walked into changed;

the tension dissipated, and the men started to talk of the farm, their plans for the rest of the week, and finally Sam said, 'So, you've employed someone?'

'Wow! Your listening skills are impressive,' I teased him. 'You can be mesmerised with your phone and still understand what is being said.'

He raised his middle finger, and we both laughed.

'Laura is thirtyish and is a single mum. Her husband died a couple of years ago, and she is just starting to get back on her feet. Her son, Toby, started school this year, and she wants something that will suit school hours. That's fine by me, I just want someone reliable. She's going to work with me for a week or so, but you'll meet her when she comes to get some supplies.'

Idle chatter saw us all calm and relaxed through dessert and beyond. It was nice, the best evening we had spent together since the detectives had paid us a visit.

'Who wants coffee?' asked Mum.

'I'll make it,' I offered. 'You go and sit on the verandah and relax. I'll bring it out.' I then turned to my brothers. 'And if you promise to wash up later, I've got some chocolates in my room, and I just might share them with you.'

*

The night air was cool, fragrant, and it eddied around Mum and I as we sat; she with another coffee, and me with a glass of wine. Uncle Arthur had joined Sam and Max in the kitchen – it was his way of giving us space to talk.

'I saw Ant today,' I told her, leaving the question hanging in the air between us.

'I told Sam and Max. They're okay with it. It's … what triggered your father leaving all those years ago. That's why I told him to leave. Mind you, there is more to it than that, love, but honestly, I've had enough talking about it for one day. Can we just leave it for now?'

'Sure,' I replied. I was happy to wait. I had learnt enough secrets recently to know that often they were born from pain or shame, as well as wanting to protect.

A pleasant silence connected us – the words would come later.

The next few days drifted by slowly with our usual routines filling our time. Laura came as promised, and Toby and Sam had an immediate connection. He had never wanted children or showed any interest in the ones with whom he had had contact, so it was a surprise to everyone.

Laura proved to be hard-working, good company and reliable.

Ant and I met every day in the park; there had been no plans made for the brothers to get together, and while it wasn't what we wanted, both Ant and I accepted it. His relationship with his mother was still strained. Ant spent very little time on the station, and I suspected that was because he wanted to spend as little time with her as possible. My tolerance to family secrets was at an all-time low – I didn't want to hear any more – so I was happy to wait until somebody was ready to talk.

The day Ant flew back to Sydney was hard. A piece of my heart went with him. Loneliness settled over me like a cloud, and I found it hard to shake.

One afternoon, a car followed me home. It was one I had seen before, so I wasn't surprised when Sergeant Law and his sidekick Constable Drury alighted from the car.

I stared at them both for a moment, thinking *shit, now what*, then I turned without saying a word and made my way inside the house.

They followed me. They didn't seem to be in the mood for polite greetings either.

Mum, ever the host, settled the men on the couch. This time, they accepted a cup of coffee, and Mum placed a plate of biscuits within their reach. They looked like they were settling in for a long stay.

We gathered around and waited.

Sergeant Law took a sip of his coffee, opened his mouth as if to speak, and then Uncle Arthur wandered in; his timing, as ever, was eerie. The dogs followed him in and found comfortable spots to rest and watch.

Introductions over, Sergeant Law began, 'The DNA results show that the body is indeed Lincoln Kelly.'

Sam let out a whoosh of air, and Max said, 'I told you.'

We all looked at them, but they didn't elaborate, and no one asked any questions.

Sergeant Law glanced around as if expecting another sort of reaction. When there was no visible response, he continued, 'The death is suspicious because of the location in which he was found, and as yet, no cause of death has been determined, but that investigation is still in progress.'

'I don't know why you think the location of his death is suspicious. Lincoln was more than capable of throwing himself into that gully just to make it look suspicious. Anyway, thank you for letting us know, Detective,' said Mum, her tone indicating the visit was over. She started to rise from her chair.

'We would like to ask some further questions?' He phrased it as a question, but I knew it was a statement.

Clearly unhappy, Mum sank slowly back into the chair.

'Okay, fire away,' said Uncle Arthur.

'Can you tell us why your husband left.'

'Because we had an argument, and I told him to.'

'What day was this exactly?'

'It was twenty years ago. I don't remember the exact date, but it was just before Christmas ... December sometime.'

Sergeant Law studied the notes in his hand. 'December fifteenth, the same day your son Sam and you were admitted to hospital.'

Mum stared at him. A small gasp had escaped her lips, and then I saw her lips tighten, clamp together.

'Doctors are required to report suspicious injuries, Ms Ayres, especially in children.' He glanced at Sam.

Horrified, I looked at Mum. 'Mum? What ... is he talking about?'

She shook her head at me as if to say, 'not now'.

I glanced at everyone in the room, and no member of my family would meet my eyes.

Sergeant Law kept his gaze firmly on Mum. 'Ms Ayres …' he prompted, before again studying his notes.

I had the distinct impression he knew exactly what was in those notes.

He cleared his throat and took another mouthful of coffee before saying, 'Okay, then. You were treated for severe concussion and contusions to the head, and Samuel, who was eight years old at the time, was treated for severe lacerations to the body, mainly the torso … caused, it says here, from barbwire and … from being whipped.'

The story Shirley told me rushed to the forefront of my mind. Had she known that it had been about Sam? Could it have been her way of warning me that there were more secrets? While I felt shocked at first, I had not really entertained it as a reality affecting my family; instead, I chose to believe the story Sam had told about falling off a horse.

All of a sudden, I felt hot, then icy fingers crept up my spine, and the room started to blur.

A hand gently touched the back of my head, pushing it down, and I heard Uncle Arthur say, 'Put your head between your legs until it passes.'

Sergeant Law clearly wasn't concerned that I was about to pass out; he continued talking.

*Prick.*

'I have the police report from that time here, Ms Ayres, but now I'm investigating a probable murder and would like to hear it from you. Can you tell me what the argument was about?'

'It was about his treatment of the children. When I told him to leave, he became violent, and I ... I hit him with a chair, then I fled out of the house. I was yelling at the boys to get in the car when Lincoln tackled me and knocked me to the ground. Then he started punching me, and I blacked out. When I came to, it was late afternoon and at first, I had trouble finding the boys, but eventually, I found Sam. He ... was tangled up in the barbwire, and Lincoln had taken a whip to him. He was unconscious and bleeding. I got him free and carried him up to the car. I couldn't find Max. But I needed to get Sam to hospital, and I just hoped that ...' Mum took a deep breath. Her voice was wobbly, and tears were flowing freely down her face. 'He was safe.'

She then finished in a whisper, 'I had to leave him, I had to get Sam to hospital.'

It was the plea for understanding that broke my heart. I sat up and took some deep breaths.

'Did anyone help you?' Sergeant Law asked.

'Stop! Stop!' I cried, tears streaming down my face. 'We need a break. Can't you see how upsetting all this is.'

Uncle Arthur touched my arm. 'Let her finish. It needs to be said.'

'Yes. I drove to Fletcher Thompson's place. They helped dress Sam's wounds, and then Nicole drove Sam and I into the hospital, which at that time was two hours away. Fletcher went looking for Max.'

Sergeant Law nodded and turned his attention to Max. 'You were six years old at the time. Can you tell us what you remember.'

'I remember ...' Max paused, then with contempt showing clearly in his face and voice ... '*Him* ... punching Mum. Sam and I hit the bastard with sticks to try and stop him. But he turned on us, and we ran. Sam got caught up in the barbwire fence. He started punching Sam at first ... then ... he ... he ... just stopped suddenly and walked away. I was trying to help Sam out of the wire when we saw him coming back with a whip in his hand. That's when Sam started yelling at me to run. So, I did.'

'Did your father find you?'

'No. But he came close. I remember running up the road and him gunning the motorbike.'

'He had a motorbike?'

'Yes.'

'Was there a motorbike with the body?' asked Uncle Arthur.

Sergeant Law's glance at Uncle Arthur said, 'I'm asking the questions.' He turned his eyes back onto Max. 'What else can you remember?'

'I remember the motorbike stopped. Then it started again, and he rode away.'

'You remember it leaving?'

'Yeah, I remember that because it meant he wasn't chasing me anymore, and I was relieved.'

'Where did you go?'

'I went back and hid in the shed, just in case he was trying to trick me.'

'What happened then?'

'The next thing I remember is Mr Thompson calling me. He took me home, and he gave me the best hot chocolate I've ever tasted. I don't know what was in it, but I've never had another hot chocolate like it.'

There was something in Max's voice that made us all grin; even the detectives couldn't hide their smiles.

'Did you ever ask him?' I asked.

'Sure, and he said, "secret ingredient".' Max winked at me, which told me he knew exactly what the ingredient was.

'Do you remember how long after you heard your father ride away that Mr Thompson found you?'

'No.'

'Did Mr Thompson stay with you?'

'He was asleep on the floor beside me when I woke up. Snoring, very loudly. I remember that.'

Sergeant Law turned to Uncle Arthur. 'Where were you at this time?'

'Not here. I didn't come until a few weeks later.'

'Can you verify that?'

'It was twenty years ago, mate. Who's going to remember where I was?'

'I can,' said Mum quietly.

'So can I,' Sam and Max said in unison, and they grinned at each other.

With a glance at his fellow officer, Sergeant Law

closed his folder and rose to his feet. 'Thank you for your time and the coffee. We'll be in touch.'

The following morning, I hit the alarm and wished I wasn't self-employed. I wanted to sleep late, go for a long walk and eat chocolate. Anything other than work.

Instead, I dragged myself out of bed and mooched out to the kitchen. Mum had coffee ready, as well as toast; I lathered on the butter, added a smear of vegemite and munched away.

'You okay, sweetheart?'

I met her eyes and nodded.

'We didn't tell you because …'

'I know, Mum. I know … you wanted to protect me. But you see, you didn't. You all just left me out of the inner circle. Even Uncle Arthur knew, didn't he?'

'Most of it, yes,' she said quietly.

There was nothing more to say. I had a lot to process. I finished the last of the coffee and toast and pushed away from the table. 'I have to go to work, Mum. I'll see you tonight.'

*

I had given Laura her own clients, and we both worked solo, unless it was a job for two; so, I was alone to brood during my work hours. Mum and Max's words continued to replay in my head.

A kaleidoscope of emotions accompanied the memories Mum, Sam and Max had divulged of that night, and I felt battered by them.

I'd noticed no one had mentioned Lincoln being Anthony's father, which meant they were afraid suspicion would land at Mr Thompson's door, but I figured it would anyway, since he was, apart from Max, one of the last people to see Lincoln alive.

That afternoon, I called in on Shirley. I didn't want to go home. I wanted peace away from all the turmoil and secrets. I also wanted to feel that I belonged, and I didn't with a family who, in the name of protection, had excluded me from so much. While their protection had given me a wonderful childhood, it had placed me outside the family. I knew there were still secrets, but I no longer wanted to know them.

Shirley greeted me warmly, and we sat in her kitchen, ate scones, drank tea and talked of everything except family. If Shirley sensed I wasn't happy, she didn't pry.

After a while, the words petered out and we sat in a comfortable silence, it was like a warm embrace. I inhaled deeply and let it out in a long sigh.

'Time to go then,' suggested Shirley, and I nodded.

As I was leaving, Shirley gave me a quick, firm hug, and I knew she had seen my unhappiness, seen me, and so I was ready to re-enter my family.

## Chapter Thirteen

# Fletcher

Fletcher watched the cop car drive away. Questions had been asked and answered, some truthfully, some, by omission, not.

The big question was, did they believe him?

The evening he and Nicole heard a car pull up outside their house was etched in his memory. He went out to see who it was to find Kate, bruised, bloody and vomiting beside the car. She gestured towards the car with a weak wave, and he found Sam in an even worse condition. The boy was still unconscious, and the cabin of the car looked like an abattoir – there was blood everywhere.

Fletcher lifted the boy from the car and carried him inside. 'See to Kate,' he told his wife. He then laid Sam on the table and felt like vomiting himself.

Deep lacerations covered his entire torso, some would need stitches, and he had lost a considerable amount of blood. Bruises covered his head and chest. Both eyes had swelled shut.

Kate haltingly told them her tale of horror while he and Nicole dressed Sam's wounds.

'I've left Max there. I've left Max there.' Kate sobbed over and over.

Nicole fetched a glass of water and helped Kate lift it to her lips.

'I'll find him, Kate. I'll find him,' Fletcher reassured her.

'Nicole can take Anthony and drive you and Sam to the hospital. And I'll go and find him and bring him back.'

An hour later, his wounds dressed, Sam had regained consciousness.

Kate was calmer and had been able to drink a cup of hot, sweet tea and not vomit.

He saw them safely on their way and made his own preparations.

The moon glowed large and round in the night sky; Fletcher drove with the headlights of the car on until he crossed the causeway at the river, which signalled the end of his property and the start of Kate's land.

Once past the causeway, he turned the headlights off, stepped out of the car and allowed his eyes to adjust.

He listened: the distant sound of a motorbike; a dingo howled closer; other sounds, unidentified, reached him.

He stepped back into the car.

Fletcher wound the car windows down to allow him to hear better. The night air brushed his face, and he inhaled deeply as he wended his way slowly through the bush track that served as a road. It was clearly defined in the moonlight, and while he thought he was too far away for Max to suddenly pop out of the bush, he didn't want to take any chances.

The thrum of the motorbike was getting closer.

Fletcher drove the car off the track, turned the engine off and stepped out into the cool night air; he closed the car door quietly. In his hand, he carried a torch but didn't switch it on – he could see well enough in the moonlight, and he didn't want to alert anyone to his presence, certainly not Lincoln. If he could get the boy away without Kelly knowing, all the better; the police could deal with that mongrel.

Soft-footed, Fletcher made his way down the left-hand side of the road, stopping every now and then to listen and watch.

The sound of the motorbike was closer; he could see the headlights weaving in and out of the bush. However, he was too far away to see if there was anyone in front of the headlights being chased. It actually looked as if the motorbike rider was searching. *No doubt it's that bastard.*

Then Fletcher saw movement near the bush on the other side of the road ahead. He studied the area for a moment, not sure what he had seen; a brief shifting of a cloud and the moonlight revealed a small figure huddled in the shadows.

Max was hiding behind a tree on the right-hand side of the road. Fletcher opened his mouth to call when the motorbike gained speed on the road, and he watched as the headlights made its way to where Max was hiding.

Abruptly, Max left his hiding place and ran up the road. The headlights picked him out clearly, and the sudden roar of the engine told Fletcher that the motorbike rider had also seen the small figure running for his life.

Then suddenly …

*What the hell*, Fletcher thought.

When the motorbike reached the tree where Max had been hiding, it came to a sudden stop, and in the moonlight, Fletcher saw the rider's body catapult over the handlebars of the bike and fly through the air to land heavily on the ground with a thud and a strangled scream.

Max had now stopped running, he was close, and Fletcher could hear his ragged breathing and sobs tearing from his throat; then the small boy tore off through the bush back towards the homestead.

Fletcher approached the rider slowly. Harsh breaths and groaning. He was alive. Fletcher stopped near him and watched as the rider turned slowly over. Protruding from the side of Lincoln's throat was a small stick, which the impact of his fall had forced into his neck. Fletcher switched the torch on then squatted in the dust beside Kelly and examined the wound.

Lincoln's hand reached up to grab the stick.

'Pull that out, mate, and your dead,' Fletcher told him. 'It looks like it's hit the artery.'

The wound had started to leak blood, and Lincoln's neck was visibly swelling. Blood was pooling inside and around the entry point of the injury. Fletcher figured soon the swelling would cut off his airway.

'Help me,' whispered Lincoln.

Fletcher tried to find some pity for the man lying on the ground in front of him; however, the trouble was images of Kate and Sam as he last saw them, bruised and bloody from Lincoln's cruelty, kept appearing in front of his eyes. And as much as he loved the son he had been given, the price he and Nicole's relationship had paid for this man's malice had been too high.

Instead, contempt was the only emotion he could find, and he said, 'Nuh, you should pull it out, mate. You'll die quicker that way.' Fletcher stood and made his way over to where the bike was resting. The motor was silent. He then stood for several heartbeats looking at what had caused Lincoln to fly over the bike. His mind struggled to comprehend what he was seeing.

*Oh shit! Oh SHIT!*

That's why the boy was standing behind the tree. He was waiting.

Across the road, strung between two trees was a line of fencing wire. Max was small and couldn't string it very high, but it was just high enough to catch the bike and fling its rider off.

The boy had set a trap, used himself as bait and waited.

Using his torch, Fletcher examined the trees.

Serrations, where the wire had cut into the bark, showed unmistakeably in the torchlight.

The decision was made subconsciously.

Fletcher didn't hesitate.

He hauled the bike from under the wire, mounted and kickstarted it. Then he rode the bike past the body of the dying man, and past his car to the boundary of the two properties, where he hid it behind a large dead eucalyptus and covered the bike with branches.

Fletcher then jogged back to his vehicle and drove it to the wire.

A quick look at Lincoln told Fletcher he was dead; he had pulled the stake from his neck and exsanguinated rather than die from asphyxiation. He must have realised, at some point, that those were his choices and knew that help, for him, would never come.

Taking a pair of wire cutters from the tools he carried in his car, Fletcher removed the wire from the trees and threw it into the back of the car.

He drove slowly to Kate's house, a plan taking shape in his mind.

The moon's light revealed a hushed landscape that both revealed and concealed.

*Where is the boy? Watching from the shadows?*

Fletcher stood beside the car, listened and heard nothing.

He made his way to the house and collected clothes from each of the bedrooms. Kate and the boys would need a change of clothes, and from Lincoln's wardrobe, he chose a set of overalls and a pair of boots. The rest of what he needed he would get from the shed. In case the body was ever discovered, he would need to ensure that only Lincoln's DNA was found.

He threw the bag of clothes into the car and yelled, 'Max! Max! It's Fletcher Thompson.' He called several times and waited.

Finally, a faint shuffle caught his attention, and he turned towards the shed.

A small figure appeared, dirty, scuffed and Fletcher could see that each step Max took was filled with trepidation. Something glinted in the little boy's hand, giving Fletcher pause and making him hesitate before approaching.

Fletcher squinted, looked more closely and saw that in his fist, Max clutched a knife. Fletcher squatted on his haunches and said softly, 'Your dad's gone, son. You can put the knife down now.'

Silence.

The boy stared at him, unblinking, and Fletcher worried that his mind was balanced on a knife's edge.

'Your Mum and Sam are alive. Nicole, you remember Nicole. She and little Anthony took them to hospital. They're going to be okay.'

'They're … okay,' Max whispered. The blank stare left his eyes and a speck of light showed briefly before it was gone.

Fletcher took a deep breath and waited for Max to process. 'Can you put the knife down? I'll take you home to my place, and in the morning, I'll take you to see your mum and Sam. Nod if that's okay.'

A long silence.

A small nod.

'Let it go, Max, and I'll pick it up,' Fletcher said gently.

The knife slipped from Max's grasp and lay in the dirt at his feet. The little boy stood unmoving.

*Is he also unseeing*, thought Fletcher. 'Is it all right if I come closer?'

Silence.

Another nod.

Fletcher scooted forward until he was almost touching the boy. 'Can I hug you?

He opened his arms and slowly wrapped them around the little body.

A strong smell of urine wafted upwards.

Time passed, and the little boy in his arms slowly, ever so slowly, relaxed.

Fletcher changed position then and sat in the dirt, cradling the child. Finally, he heard a soft sigh escape Max's lip and felt the small body – again, ever so slowly – relax into his arms. 'I'm going to stand up now and we're going to get in the car and drive to my place. Is that okay.'

A nod.

On the way home, Fletcher kept Max close to his side and reassured him as he drove that tonight Max would sleep at his house, and in the morning, they would go and see his mum and Sam. Fletcher repeated it until he stopped the car in front of his house.

Max didn't protest when Fletcher showered him and dressed him in the clothes he had found in the bedrooms.

He led the silent child to the couch and wrapped him in a blanket. It was summer, but the boy was shivering, and Fletcher figured that that had nothing to do with the climate.

'Would you like a hot chocolate?'

Another nod.

Fletcher made the hot chocolate and laced it with half a nip of chocolate rum liqueur and lots of sugar.

Max sipped at the drink. 'Umm.'

'You like it?'

A nod.

'Good, I made myself one too.' Fletcher sat beside Max on the couch and watched him. When he had finished the drink and his eyes were slowly closing, Fletcher eased him down and covered him.

He figured he had four hours before Max's sleep would lighten and he might stir and, in that time, he had a body and a motorbike to hide.

## Chapter Fourteen

# Detective Sergeant Neil Law

'What do you reckon, Sarge,' asked Constable James Drury as he steered the car slowly over the bumpy road.

Sergeant Neil Law grimaced. 'I reckon the story he told about finding that kid nearly broke my fucking heart.' Though, he figured anything involving kids broke his heart.

'Yeah. Poor bloody kid. His father must have got close to catching him for him to piss himself.'

'Hmm,' was the only reply from Sergeant Neil Law. He was deep in thought, watching with unseeing eyes the passing bush; instead, he was envisioning a small boy running for his life and hiding from a man who was supposed to love him. How horrible must it have been to have had a father like Lincoln Kelly.

'He seems to have turned out all right,' Drury's words punctured the picture in Law's head, and he turned his head to look at the man beside him.

'On the surface, yes. I've checked and neither of them have been in trouble with the law. Apart from them being almost thirty and still living with their mother, they do seem "normal"', Law replied.

Drury chuckled. 'Yeah, I know what you mean. I couldn't live with my parents anymore. Though, mind you, it's not Dad, it's bloody Mum.' He turned onto the main road into town. 'Do you think we've got a case?' he asked after a few kilometres had rushed past.

Law glanced at his partner. 'Tell me what you think.'

'Well. The only DNA we have is Kelly's. There was nothing else found on anything recovered from the gully. The pathologist said he died by "exsanguination", because of the amount of blood found on the few pieces of clothing that were at the scene. No murder weapon. And there was only a tiny piece of wood lodged in the cervical spine. Which could mean he was stabbed with a piece of wood or fell on a piece. But we haven't found the motorbike that both the boy and Thompson claimed he was riding. And they both stated he left on the bike,' said Drury.

'It could have been anyone riding that bike. Thompson said he assumed it was Kelly because he had seen the lights weaving in and out of the trees,' interjected Law. 'So, it looked like someone was looking for something or someone.' He paused, stared out the window before resuming. 'The officer who investigated twenty years ago was happy to accept that Kelly had left. It makes sense because Kelly would have known he would have been taken into custody for what he did to the older boy.'

'The mother could be right. Kelly could have done it himself,' suggested Drury.

'But what did he do with the motorbike?'

'Threw it in the river, then hiked back to the gully.'

Law shook his head. 'No, that river gets pretty low, and it's flooded a few times over the years. I think the bike would have surfaced by now if it was in the river.' He scratched his chin then added. 'And if Thompson did get rid of it, I reckon he would have stripped it into parts and hid it in plain sight. Believe me, it's gone.'

'You didn't want to share the cause of death with the family or Thompson?' suggested Drury.

'No. I wanted to see what their stories were first. See if anyone might let anything slip.'

'Are you going to tell them?' asked Drury.

'Sure. In time. Or the coroner will.'

'What about the Crown?'

'I'll write my report, run it past Lucy; she's the boss. The final decision is hers, but the truth is we have no evidence. I doubt that the Crown will touch it.'

'I doubt they will either. After hearing their stories, between you and me, whatever happened, that prick got off lightly,' said Drury.

Law nodded his agreement. Initially, he had been appalled by the thought of Kelly's body being dumped in a gully and left to rot, and though he would never say it out loud, he now figured the man got what he deserved. He was just glad they hadn't found any evidence against the family or … Thompson, the only one out of all of them who would have been capable at the time of disposing of a body and a motorbike.

## Chapter Fifteen

# Jane

The months passed with the changing of the seasons. Officially, spring had ended, though the first days of summer were still cool. Christmas was already being advertised. The business was busier than ever; Laura proved to be a godsend, and I had recently been thinking that maybe I should hire another person to help.

I continued to see Sergeant Law occasionally in passing. We'd nod at each other but never speak. Another time we might have been friends ... or more. There was a frisson of something between us, but I doubted either of us would ever act on it. I would have to introduce him to *all* my brothers, and that would raise questions that no one, least of all me, would want to answer.

It seemed that I too had chosen: silence.

For a couple of months now, Laura and Sam had been taking Toby to watch children's movies. However, they finally decided to see an adult movie sans Toby and have asked Mum to babysit.

Sam told me he was worried about what kind of a father he would make, and I told him not to be so bloody stupid; he raised me, didn't he. He would make a wonderful father. I saw understanding touch his eyes and relief relax his body. He would not be the parent Lincoln had been.

Max was building, with Uncle Arthur's help, and sometimes Sam – when he could tear himself away from Laura – a cabin in the woods. His scars weren't visible, but they ran deeper than Sam's, and while I thought about that sometimes, I never asked. Some things were best not to know.

Another kind of silence, I decided.

Fletcher Thompson – call me 'Fletcher', he told me, and I did, sometimes, though I liked the formality of calling him Mr Thompson, as it provided an invisible barrier that I liked to keep between us – was spending more and more time with Mum. Their friendship was a rock for them both, and often I wished it had been something more. That we had had him for a father.

Nicole was now living in town. It seemed like she had broken out of some sort of self-imposed prison. She had become a party girl (or woman), much to the horror (or delight) of the town gossips. It seemed to me she lived a life that had been decided by others and now she was exploring ways in which she wanted to live her own life. I knew better than to judge; no one knew the silence and secrets that laid in the stories of others.

Even though I tracked down my real grandmother – Hazel – I decided I didn't want to get to know her after all.

Margaret Kelly, who I now referred to as 'Great-Aunt Kelly', I saw occasionally, and we have started to smile and acknowledge each other in passing. The other day, I said hello as I passed her in the street and she responded. Maybe there was hope, but I was happy to accept what is.

I had been living in a townhouse for a couple of months and found that while I missed the bush, I enjoyed having my own space. It had three bedrooms;

one I used as an office and the other was a spare for whoever wanted to crash for the night or longer.

Ant was coming home soon, and he was staying with me, and I found I was looking forward to having a brother who didn't carry the deep scars that my other brothers did. Selfish, perhaps. But recently, a figurative bomb had exploded the life I knew, and I was trying to cobber the pieces to together and build a new life.

I figured I was allowed some selfishness.

Lincoln's bones were released for burial. A soft wind played with fallen leaves and swirled them around our feet as we walked towards the grave site.

Only five people attended: Uncle Arthur, Mum, Fletcher, Great-Aunt Kelly and I stood beside the gravesite and watched the coffin being lowered in silence. There was no priest or celebrant to conduct funeral rites and certainly no eulogy to celebrate his life.

Great-Aunt Kelly was the only one who cried. I couldn't imagine that those tears were for the man, so I figured they must have been for the boy she loved and raised. Then another thought occurred to me: when she discovered the child she loved was not only her sister's, but her husband's, and that they abandoned her and the child, on whom did she take out her anger and frustration? The sister, the husband, or the little boy.

Perhaps her tears were for more than what they seemed.

As we walked away, Mum and Fletcher joined hands, and united they made their way to the cars.

Sudden tears flooded my eyes and prickled my nose, and I couldn't help thinking about opportunities lost.

We met up, after the funeral, in the park. It seemed as good a place as any to hold a quasi-wake. Only we weren't there to remember, we gathered to say goodbye and forget.

Mum and I sat at the table in a comfortable silence. I had gotten over feeling sorry for myself. I realised that while they had kept their secrets, which excluded me, I had been given a happy childhood, free of the fear, doubt and worry that must have been so much a part of Mum's and my brothers' lives.

As well as being her daughter, I had found a friendship with my mother, which was infinitely better.

Uncle Arthur and Fletcher had wandered off, and I went to find them to tell them Mum and I were ready to go.

They were on the other side of the large camphor laurel tree that I had stood Ant under many moons ago and told him to steady himself.

Their words floated back to me.

Uncle Arthur seemed to be replying to something Fletcher had said.

'I've always believed his mind was protecting him from something, and now because of all that's happened, Max's memories have been tossed in the air, and they are forming images he's not sure are true. His nightmares are getting worse.'

Silence fell between the two men, and I waited on the other side of the tree, feeling tension build inside of me, caught between wanting to listen and the fear of hearing too much.

'I'm not sure I can help,' Fletcher eventually replied. 'Some things are best left unsaid. Once spoken, they can take on a life of their own.'

'The body carries its own memories. I believe the nightmares are a way of revealing what his mind can't accept.' As ever, Uncle Arthur's voice was mild but held steel and conviction.

'Maybe it's best if he doesn't know the truth?' countered Fletcher.

'He can only heal if he knows the truth, and while I'm still alive to help him.' Uncle Arthur's voice was now firm, knowing.

'You don't know what you are asking. Silence is the best protection I can offer.'

'Silence in this instance may do more harm than good. You have my word that whatever you say will stay between just the three of us.'

My mind seemed to go blank, and my breath caught somewhere deep inside my chest as I waited behind the tree, afraid of what I might hear nor wanting the men to know that I listened, but also seemingly unable to move.

After another long silence, Fletcher replied, 'When he is ready … and he is sure that this is what he wants, let me know and I'll talk to you both.'

'Thank you.'

Loath to hear any more secrets, I forced myself to move. I walked around the tree and faced them. They clearly knew that I had heard, but I didn't ask questions, and they didn't provide any answers.

Perhaps I too now understood both the destructiveness and the value of silence.

# Acknowledgements

I wrote the first draft of *Silence Has Many Faces* in three months, it took another ten months to get it to publication.

So many people help in the creation of a novel from first draft to completion and I would like to thank those who helped me.

Feedback from my daughter Jenny encouraged me to rewrite chapter nine and it is all the better for the rewriting.

Michele Perry, from Wordplay Editing Service has once again helped me polish and refine a manuscript.

Betty Rimmington, a fellow author, pointed out my overuse of the word 'had' which encouraged me to write better sentences.

Ann Dettori, of Independent Ink wrote the back blurb for me, thank you Ann and also to your team who have assisted in the creation of the finished product.